FAERY PROPHET

FAERY CHRONICLES BOOK TWO

LESLIE CLAIRE WALKER

sfp

FAERY PROPHET

Rude Davies is everyone's friend, the life of the party with unusually good luck—and an epic secret...

No one can know that Rude has joined the Faery underground hidden in the shadows of the city. But he can't hide how much he loves to help people—especially oddballs and outcasts. So, when a disquieting girl calls for magical aid, he answers—and discovers that she and her supernatural demon emergency are way out of his league.

Rude must assemble and lead bold friends and brave allies in the fight to triumph over evil. There's just one small problem: If Rude can't summon enough daring to face his own demons, he risks becoming one himself.

ALSO BY LESLIE CLAIRE WALKER

THE AWAKENED MAGIC SAGA

THE SOUL FORGE

(The Complete Series)

Angel Hunts

Angel Rises

Angel Falls

Angel Strikes

Angel Roars

Angel Burns

THE FAERY CHRONICLES

(The Complete Series)

Faery Novice

Faery Prophet

Faery Sovereign

SHORT STORY COLLECTIONS

Ink & Blood

Ink & Stars

Ink & Sword

CHAPTER 1

I T WAS A STICKY September Saturday night in Houston, Texas, on a sidewalk outside of the Rollins Pub, where Johnny Rocket played his thunder bass. People in various stages of inebriation mingled and the stink of stale beer lingered. Not the normal hangout spot for a sober dude without a fake ID. But, hey, I had responsibilities and a mostly secret identity.

My name? Rudolph Diamond Davies III. Rude, to my friends. Unofficially, the class clown. The party guy. The one with the uncanny luck. Always ready to be a friend or help out a dude in need. My official assignment: Save life. Prevent death. And other bad things.

I leaned against the brick wall outside the pub and stared at the old oak on the other side of the walk. Anyone else would see an ordinary tree whose ordinary roots buckled the sidewalk—if they noticed it at all. Me? I saw a portal to and from the Otherworld.

Otherworld, as in the place where faeries, demons, and angels lived. Sometimes they traveled through portals, aka gates, into the human realm. Sometimes they even came with good intentions.

I had it on good authority, however, that a visitor planned to bust through tonight, bleeding bad vibes and looking for trouble. As the youngest (and only) faery seer apprentice to the (only) full seer in town, I'd use my magic to turn them around. Send them back.

I kept my gaze on the tree. Didn't even blink. Until I spotted a girl I knew from senior English out of the corner of my eye.

Melody. Pretty name for a cheerleader-next-door kind of girl. Wavy blond hair brushed her shoulders. Her blue eyes sparkled when she saw me. I didn't know what to do except smile. And stare.

She didn't look like herself.

She wore red stilettos so tall and sharp, they practically sparked on the pavement. A short black skirt swung high on her thighs and a white tank hugged her every considerable curve. Definitely different clothes than she wore Monday through Friday.

Her cheekbones seemed a little high and sharp. Her mouth looked more severe. A worry line had erupted in the center of her forehead.

It wasn't just the clothes and the changes in her face that bothered me, though. She had a halo around her body the color of mud. What psychics would call a bad aura. A portent of violence—against herself or someone else? Either way, worry-making.

She pulled a pack of smokes from a tiny black purse and lit one as she sidled up to me. She elbowed me in the ribs, trying to be playful and failing—because that worry line? It didn't go away.

"Hey, Rude," she said in her husky voice.

"Hey, yourself. Didn't think I'd see you here."

"Same goes. What are you up to?"

"Holding up the wall," I said. Not exactly a lie. "Too bad I can't get in. Johnny Rocket's sounding real good. What I can hear of him, anyway."

She laughed. The line in her brow stayed through that, too. "How is it that a guy who throws the best keg parties in town—parties that practically the entire school comes to—doesn't have an ID for some-place like this?"

"I plead innocence."

"You?"

"Yeah, me. Really. You feeling okay?"

"Do I look like I have a fever or something?" She leaned in close, I guess so I could feel her forehead and give my best non-MD opinion. So close I could smell her subtle rose perfume. And underneath it, something stranger.

A sickly sweet scent, like cough syrup. And sulfur.

I took a deep breath to be sure and blew it out slow.

"Well?" she asked.

"You seem like you're in trouble." I thought twice about remarking on the smells, but the way she looked? I had to know, and the best way to do that was to use the element of vocal surprise. Best-case scenario, she'd just think I was weird. I was okay with that. Worst case? I hoped we didn't go there.

So I said, "And you smell like a demon."

Her eyes narrowed. "That's not nice."

I hadn't meant it to be, exactly. I held her gaze.

She fidgeted under my über-scrutiny.

"I repeat: trouble. What's up, Melody? I can help."

"No faery seer apprentice can help me," she said. But not convincingly. Spoken like somebody fishing for confirmation or information.

I'd wanted her to spill her guts about the problem. Or if something had possessed her (hey, it happened), it might un-possess her and run. I hadn't expected her to spout off about my extracurricular activities. She shouldn't have known.

My turn to fidget. "Will you tell me what you mean by that?"

She took a drag on her smoke. Her fingers trembled. "I have a confession. I didn't come here to see Johnny Rocket. I came to see you."

"How?"

"I took the bus."

"No," I said. "How did you know where to find me?"

"I've been having some seriously screwed-up feelings lately. I'm angry all the time."

"You have a lot to be pissed off about."

She held my gaze. "You know?"

"Look, people talk. You know that. I heard some stuff at school."

"From?"

"It's not important, Melody."

"The hell it's not. Probably those girls pretending to be my *friends*." She raised her hands and made air quotes for emphasis.

I nodded. One person's private tragedy could become another person's juicy gossip. In Melody's case, the gossip went like this: Her stepfather beat the crap out of her. She showed up at school with a sunrise of bruises and two black eyes about a month ago. She left home. Went to stay with Beth Barrett, everyone's favorite science fiction geek, for a couple of days that turned into a more permanent arrangement.

The stepdad had been arrested and then let go because neither Melody's mom nor Melody pressed charges. Mom loved him more than she loved her own daughter. And he terrified Melody.

Although the people at school talked about all this like it'd been a one-time thing, I had my doubts.

"Those girls who started the rumors are assholes," I said.

"Thanks," she said. "This anger thing? It's not about him. It's not even about my mother. It's like power surges or something. I can't control when it happens. I can barely keep from punching my fist through the wall. And I know stuff. It just pops into my head. Like what you are. And where to find you—like I could..."

"What?"

She hesitated. "Smell you. From all the way across town."

"The only people I know who can do that aren't human. But you are."

"Not entirely."

I blinked at her.

She flushed. "I know it sounds crazy."

"No."

"Maybe not to you. You're a freak who hangs out with other freaks." She sucked in a breath. "No offense."

I tried not to take any. After all, it was kind of accurate. "So if you're not one-hundred-percent human, what else are you?"

The words tumbled out fast and low, for my ears only. "Demon, I think. Like you said."

I couldn't think of a worse thing. Not one. "How?"

"I found some stuff in my mom's diary. Stuff about my real dad. I was looking for money, you know? Sometimes she hides bills in there. I mean, she hasn't written anything in it for years, but she still keeps it. And it says outright that my actual dad wasn't human. That she had suspicions when she met him, but she didn't find out for sure until after I was born. She said my eyes were red, Rude. They turned blue, the way other kids' eyes start out blue when they're born and then turn brown."

I studied her face. She didn't seem to be making up any of this. She spoke the dead-on truth as she understood it. "Whoa."

"Exactly. What do I do?"

I had no idea how to answer that question. I'd heard of human and Otherworld hybrids before, but I'd never seen one. I'd certainly never met one. If I found out something like that about myself, I'd be terrified of what I might do to other people. Non-humans...well, they weren't *human*. They didn't think the same way. They didn't have the same kinds of morals.

I swallowed hard. "Did you ask your mom about it?"

"You're kidding, right?" She peered at my not-kidding face. "Okay, I kind of did. I said *so this is a joke* and she stared at me. So I said *this is like a metaphor* and she looked away from me. I said *this is real?* and she told me to get out. That was the last thing that happened before I left home."

"After your stepfather hit you."

She winced.

"Sorry. When was the last time you had an anger flash?"

"Two nights ago."

"Anything weird happen?"

"I destroyed my trash can. You know, in my room."

"Define *destroyed*."

"One second it was normal and the next it, like, melted. I

completely lost my mind. I spent the rest of the night curled up in a ball in the closet."

Holy crap. "You ever done anything like that before?"

"Two weeks ago. To the steering wheel of my car. Well, Beth's car. Her mom was so beyond mad. Which is why I took the bus."

"How many times has it happened total?" I asked.

"Twelve."

"And you didn't come to me until now?"

Her voice started out low and rose with each word. "I would've if I'd known about you before this afternoon."

Her complexion took on a red cast. This time, she didn't look embarrassed. Frustrated, maybe. Frustrated could lead to mad, which I didn't want to see. Not yet, anyway. I held up both hands to signal a truce.

She looked away. Cocked her head. "What's that?"

The bark of the oak tree had begun to shimmer. The Otherworld gate had been activated. Another thing humans couldn't usually see.

I put out my arm. Pushed her behind me.

"What?" she asked again.

"It could be dangerous," I said.

"So could I."

Well, yeah. But I had to choose my battles.

A bang and crunch behind us had me throwing a desperate glance over my shoulder. Just a couple of bouncers setting down and flipping open a chest filled with bottled water and ice.

I faced front again. A small horde of crows had landed in the branches of the tree, and the gate within the trunk had stopped shimmering and started to pulse. The brown of the bark brightened until it bled white. All the hair on my body stood straight up. Luckily, I had a buzz cut or I'd have looked like Einstein, only with orange hair.

"Jesus, Rude!" Melody whisper-shouted in my ear.

"Welcome to my world."

Just Melody and me and whoever traveled through the tree. No one else could see. The others talked and laughed. Lit smokes and, from the smell, joints. They flirted as if the world around them was safe.

The tree groaned. Split wide open to reveal a pair of thick, black lace-ups attached to two stocky legs in black pants. The being also wore a belt with a flashlight, a radio, and a gun. A cop's blue shirt, silver badge and all—official HPD wear. His arms came through next, brown and brushed with fine, black hair. I marked the pinky ring on his finger and knew him before I saw his face and met his watchful gaze.

"Officer Burns," I said.

He looked me up and down. Curled his lip as if he found Hawaiian shirts and cargo shorts and sneakers distasteful. "Rudolph Diamond Davies."

"That's 'Mr. Davies' to you."

Melody took hold of my shirt. Shook it to get my attention. "A cop?"

"No, he's just dressed like one. He's fae."

"An imposter faery cop?"

I shrugged. "I'll handle him."

Or *them*. Because where Burns went, his evil twin, Officer Reid, always followed.

Sure enough, Burns stepped away from the gate. Two seconds later, redheaded, freckled Reid stepped from the tree and onto the sidewalk, beer gut hung over his belt. He got in my face, nose-to-nose.

"We heard something getting ready to go down," he said. "The King sent us. He's concerned."

The one and only time I'd met these busters, the Faery King had ordered them to make my best friend's life a living hell. Kevin had been Joe-normal before they came on the scene. After a whole lot of imminent mortal danger, he'd ended up a go-between. A link between the human and fae races.

"Why didn't you contact Kev?"

Reid's voice rose with every word. "That was our intention. We were to go from here to his home. But you're here, so we're asking you and you're going to tell us."

Burns laid a hand on his partner's shoulder. Reid seethed, but he backpedaled two steps. Out of my immediate space.

"The King wouldn't have sent us if it weren't important," Burns said. "All the signs in our realm point to something terrible about to happen. We know it begins here. That's all we know."

His words faded into silence. Like, actual silence. Although the crowd outside the pub never noticed the gate or anyone walking out of it, they sure noticed the sudden appearance of two officers of the law. I glanced over my shoulder. Caught sight of two dudes walking away from us fast. Probably the guys with the pot. Everybody else resumed talking, only lower key than before.

I felt hot. Hotter than usual for a September night. I wiped away trickles of sweat headed for my eyes and focused on Burns again. "I have no idea what you're talking about."

He moved in front of Reid and spoke low. "What about your master? Did he say anything to you?"

I bristled at *master*. I had a teacher. Oscar. Owner of a damned good Tex-Mex restaurant by day, faery seer by night. "Just that some troublemaker would be coming here tonight."

Burns brushed his hair back from his forehead with both hands. "Nothing else?"

The way he looked and the desperate-hopeful way he asked the question had me pulling my cell from the front pocket of my shorts and texting Oscar. He didn't answer right away. Not necessarily a problem. He could be on a mission like I was, or at the club with his boyfriend, Harvard.

Melody tugged on my shirt again. "Rude? What's going on? I don't feel right."

Officer Burns sidestepped into my line of sight. "We need your full attention, Rude."

"Just a minute." I turned on my heel and got a full-on gander at Melody.

She had that frustrated, red look that'd made me nervous before the King's officers showed up. Also, a wave of heat flowed off of her. More sweat beaded at my hairline.

My heart thumped in my chest. "Is this how it felt before? When you melted the trash can and the steering wheel?"

She nodded.

"Calm down. Deep breaths." I took one myself.

She followed my example. Once. Twice. Three times. It didn't cool the heat. Her aura took on a distinctly fire-and-smoke color.

"Holy Mother," Burns said.

Melody was burning up and continuing to heat up. How long before she went nuclear? If she didn't cool down. If—

I bolted for the ice chest. I shouldered the people beside it out of the way, wrestled it off the ground, and ran back toward Melody, tripping over my sneakers and launching the ice at Melody. It rained over her in a fall of white, and most of it shattered and scattered on the concrete like pebbles. The rest hung in her hair and stuck to her clothes. Slid down her skin in melted streams that turned to steam.

Steam.

Now people stared at us. At her. One girl's laugh rose above every other noise, then cut off.

Melody pressed her hands against her eyes. Turned away.

I caught sight of something strange on her back. Something her tank top didn't cover. Black and grey on her skin. A tattoo. Since when did Melody have ink?

Since when did Melody have ink that writhed like snakes?

I took a step toward her. "Melody, look at me."

She shook her head. "The breathing isn't working."

Screw the breathing. "What's that on your back?"

She didn't answer. The heat streaming from her rose like waves rose from asphalt at high noon in August. Meltdown imminent.

Burns saw it, too. He pulled back his arm and punched her in the side of the head. Any human girl would've lost consciousness. Ended up on the ground, probably with a concussion.

Not Melody. She turned on Burns, face screwed up in fury, and kneed him in the balls. He clutched his crotch and went down.

If ice didn't work and she couldn't be knocked out, that left magic.

I could banish an Otherworld being back to its own world, but she was part human. She belonged here.

I could blunt powers. I couldn't counteract them all the way, just enough to keep them from working one hundred percent. It'd saved my life more than once. I'd ended up scarred instead of dead.

I closed my eyes. Found the still place inside my belly where my magic lived. It pooled there like water, cool and dark and deep and shining. I breathed it up. It rose along my spine, higher with each inhale, until it reached my shoulders—then it rolled along my arms into my hands. I lifted them. Pointed them toward Melody.

"Something's happening," she said.

Officer Reid looked at her. At me. He saw what I was doing. Frowned. Moved out of range of my hands. Burns crawled away.

Melody's eyes widened. "Rude. Oh, God."

"I'm trying something."

"Try faster."

The magic flowed from the center of my palms in a wash of watery light. It spilled over her, head to toe.

She shrieked. Curled in on herself.

The slap of flip-flops and a girl's voice sounded behind me. "Hey, jerk—leave her alone!"

I couldn't afford to break eye contact with Melody to look at her. I knew she couldn't see the magic. Only Melody in pain. "I'm not touching her."

Melody fought to meet my gaze. "Rude?"

"Yeah?"

"I'm sorry."

She blinked. Her eyes turned from blue to red and back again.

A wave of nausea started in the soles of my feet and sped up my legs and gut and chest and throat and head before I could take another breath. The beating of my heart became a roar of blood that filled my ears. Until the girl behind me screamed. She screamed and screamed until I thought my head would explode.

I rushed to Melody. Wrapped her in my arms. Put myself between her and everyone else. Hoped to God that if she hurt anyone, it would be me. No one else.

I held on with all I had. Her heat poured into me. Ripped the air from my lungs. I gasped for breath. Couldn't speak a word.

My knees turned to rubber. My body tipped to the left. I couldn't balance. I refused to let her go. She fell with me.

The sidewalk rushed up to meet us.

CHAPTER 2

I BREATHED IN THE SCENT of sulfur. Coughed so much my chest and throat felt full of broken glass. If I'd had anything in my stomach, I'd have thrown it up.

Instead, I opened my eyes to slits. Got a glimpse of slick, buckled concrete and a pair of empty red stilettos, one heel snapped in half.

Melody's shoes.

I planted my palms flat on the ground and pushed up to my elbows on shaky arms, expecting carnage all around. Blood and gore. Melted people everywhere. But no. As in, there was nobody but me on the sidewalk and no evidence that anyone else—human, faery, or half-demon—had ever been there at all.

I was alone.

The streetlights had gone out for the entire block. Cars had swerved from their lanes and smashed into each other. Parked vehicles at the curbs on both sides had their windows blown out. A crew cab pickup had come up over the curb and rammed into the tree with the Otherworld gate. Sliced it clean in half, which should've been impossible. The top half of the tree had punched the truck, flattening the roof and busting the windshield.

I stood up. Wobbled while my legs decided whether to hold me.

Once they'd mostly made up their mind that I could stay upright, I lurched toward the pickup and searched inside for the driver. If the impact hadn't killed him, I could pull him out.

Except he wasn't there.

Impossible again. The driver couldn't have escaped in time. What Melody had done—what the fuck had she done?—it'd happened too fast.

My brain started to glaze over, like I could pass out again any minute. I leaned toward the truck and braced my hands against the driver's door. Searing pain screamed from my fingertips. I pulled my hands back and fell onto the curb so hard, my teeth clicked together. I bit my tongue, tasted blood.

I looked at my hurt fingers. Everything except my pinkies? Lobster red, even in the dark. I couldn't see well enough to tell for sure, but I'd been burned before and these felt worse than your usual sunburn. Second-degree, maybe.

How hot did the metal on that truck have to be to cause that? Damned hot. How had it gotten that way? Melody. The only explanation. Holy ever-loving God.

I rose again, careful not to scrape my fingers, and checked all the cars in the road for people. Didn't find anyone. Didn't touch anything.

Nobody new drove by. No one came out of any of the nearby houses or businesses. No sirens rent the air.

I didn't understand. Not any of it.

Thunder rolled overhead. I glanced up at clouds moving in fast from the Gulf of Mexico, covering the moon and stars and filling the air with the scent of impending rain and salt.

I turned back the way I'd come and stopped on a dime. The pub had been reduced to piles of brick and wood, shattered glass and bent metal. I ran toward it, picking up speed with every stride, skidding at the edge of the rubble, listening for moans or cries or any sound at all, but heard only another rumble of thunder.

"Hello?" I called.

No answer.

I climbed into the wreckage with as much care as I could summon.

Found the first pile of stuff big enough to cover a person. I thought twice before touching anything with my bare skin. Took off my shirt and used it to push aside bricks and beams and electrical wiring until I got down far enough to confirm there were no people in the pile.

"Hello?" I called again.

This time, the sound of my own voice freaked me out.

I hustled out of the rubble and onto the sidewalk. Made my way to the place I'd lain on the concrete. Without the streetlights and with the clouds blocking the sky, I shouldn't have been able to pick out the exact spot by sight. But I could because the outline of my body had been bleached white on the gray walk.

Magic had knocked me on my ass. Magic had saved it, too. I'd been running a spell when Melody's mojo hit me. A spell to blunt her power. It'd worked, all right—not to stop her, but to shield me.

I hunkered down. Touched the spot with the back of my hand. It felt cold. A complete contrast compared to everything else.

I raised my wrist to my forehead. Cold there, too. And clammy.

What'd happened here? This whole block? This whole place?

Why hadn't anybody come to see what'd gone down? Why hadn't anyone come to help? Why was I the single, shell-shocked survivor?

Not *survivor*. Wrong word. Because it implied that everybody else had died. And as far as I knew, they hadn't. They'd simply vanished.

The world started to shake. No, I was the one shaking. Any second now, my legs would give and I'd collapse and maybe lose consciousness again. The thought of that happening at all—and the idea of it happening in the middle of this magic-ridden, deserted place—caused me to move again.

I walked the three blocks to where I'd parked the Explorer back when the evening and everything in it had been normal. I didn't see a soul. Once I passed block number two, though, the car windows were more or less intact. My truck sat where I'd left it, back right window cracked, but otherwise no worse for wear.

I used the unburned pinkie on my right hand to hook the keys in the left front pocket of my shorts, unlocked the door, and slid behind the wheel. The clock on the dash read 4:13 AM. It couldn't have been later than 1:00 when Melody elbowed me in the ribs with that worried look on her face. Which meant I'd been out of it for a while after she blinked and the world went pear-shaped.

I flipped on the overhead light and confirmed the second-degree burns on my fingertips. Tilted the rearview mirror so I could get a look at my face to make sure it wasn't burned or cut up. I didn't feel anything, but that could be shock. One-hundred-percent shock.

My face bore striking similarities to the extra-white spot on the sidewalk. Pale, as if I'd seen a ghost. Or lived through something apocalyptic.

I started to look away and froze.

There was nothing white about my eyes. As in, they had no whites. They were one-hundred-percent pupil, and those pupils were black.

I heard someone suck air like they couldn't get enough. Hyperventilating from zero to sixty in ten seconds. Then I realized the overachieving breather was me.

I panicked harder. Looked everywhere—anywhere—for a solution. There. On the passenger side floorboard. The paper bag filled with a peanut butter and grape jelly sandwich and chips, meant to be my middle-of-the-night snack.

I dumped the food and breathed into the bag until I could inhale and exhale steady enough to let it go. The dash clock read 4:27 AM.

My eyes were black. *Black.*

There was something wrong with me. I had no idea what. No idea what it meant. Only that I needed to find out yesterday.

I fished the cell from my right front pocket with my right pinkie and dialed Oscar's number with my knuckles. I prayed for him to pick up. He didn't. Maybe he couldn't. Maybe something awful had happened to him, too, when Melody blinked. Maybe he needed my help.

The first fat drops of rain spattered the windshield.

I turned the key in the ignition and left rubber on the road. Headed south toward Highway 69, which would take me through downtown to the 610 Loop and Oscar's house.

As soon as I drove out of the dark zone, the sky really opened up. I had to turn the wipers on high to see at all, even with working street-lamps. With every passing block, I wished I couldn't make out the empty cars crashed or left in the road. Twice, I had to get out of the Explorer and push them out of the way so I could get through. The warm rain soaked my clothes. Even my socks. The air conditioner in my car chilled me to the bone.

The houses I passed? All of them dark. Not just middle-of-the-night dark, my gut told me. Empty. Like the cars. Like whoever had been inside sleeping before The Blink had gone up in magic smoke. My rational brain kept insisting that couldn't be true. That I should stop and check for proof.

My instinct refused to let my foot off the gas unless I had no other choice. It said that I was a lot more alone than I'd figured when I came to outside the club. Possibly, the only dude left in town. And if anyone remained inside the houses, they had to be monsters. Bloodthirsty. Lying in wait for somebody dumb enough to check.

I forced myself to take a deep breath and blow it out slow before I started to hyperventilate again. It slowed my heart down, but it didn't do a thing for my jittery hands or my chattering teeth. I white-knuckled the wheel—without considering my burned fingers. It hurt so bad, I almost passed out again.

The highway loomed ahead. I fought the urge to punch it up the entrance ramp in case of more abandoned cars.

Good thing, too. I'd have rear-ended a Mustang just outside the halo of the nearest street lamp. A Mustang with a dog in the back seat.

I slammed on the brakes and gaped. The dog was huge. Some kind of sheepdog, maybe? White with black spots and hair hanging in its eyes. Both front paws pressed against the back window. Barking like crazy.

I pulled onto the shoulder. Really, I couldn't pull anyplace else. I could get by, just barely. Be back on my way to Oscar's in a heartbeat.

That dog? The first living thing I'd seen since The Blink. The Mustang's doors and windows were closed. The dog had no way out. If I left him there, he'd be trapped.

Rain pelted me like bullets as I got out and tried the 'stang's passenger door. Locked. Which meant going back to my truck for something to pop the lock, and three tries before it gave. The car smelled like the tree-shaped pine air freshener that hung from the rearview mirror and the large coffee still steaming hot in the cup holder. And the clean dog. Who looked at me like he couldn't decide whether to defend his territory.

"Hey," I said. "You want out?"

He held my gaze. The weirdest thing for a strange dog to do unless it meant to eat me for breakfast. He woofed once.

I pushed the seat forward. He pushed toward me. I backed away slow and steady. Gave him room to climb out into the rain, going from shaggy to soaked and pitiful inside a minute. All six feet of him. If he stood on his hind legs, he'd be able to rest his paws on my shoulders.

I expected him to bolt. To careen across the freeway on probably the only night he wouldn't get run over doing something like that. To become another sad, lost dog. Instead, he hugged my side. I backpedaled another step. He matched it.

He was scared. I knew exactly how he felt.

"Okay." I opened the door to the Explorer.

He bounded inside. Splattered and shook water all over the dash and the seats. Settled in at shotgun. Woofed again.

He watched every move I made as I slid back into the car, shut the door, and wiped my face. He sniffed my hand when I reached over to pet him. Let me feel around for a collar under his wet fur. Let me get close enough to read the tag.

"Zachariah?" I asked.

The dog raised a brow.

Zach's tag had an address engraved on the flipside and a last name, too. Morgan. If he had any idea what'd happened to his Morgans, he had no way to tell me.

"We can't stay here, boy."

He looked at me.

I drove away as fast as I dared. I steered around twelve cars on that stretch of 69 before I took the ramp over to the Loop. Wove around six more before I took the exit to Oscar's place. I didn't see another soul the whole time.

Oscar's one-story, red house was dark. The McMansions on either side of it, too. His lawn sprawled beneath the long, low-hanging branches of a live oak. His Honda crouched in the drive. I pulled in behind it.

I looked at Zachariah. Oscar wouldn't thank me to bring a wet, shaggy dog inside. But I couldn't leave him in the car, both because of how I'd found him and because the whole world appeared to have come down to him and me. We ran up the walk to the porch. Zach shook himself off again while I used my key in the lock. He bounded inside as soon as I pushed open the door.

The electrical switch in the middle of the entry way worked just fine. The overhead lamp flooded the space with a wash of light. Illuminated all the usual stuff—a table in a small nook that held the glass bowl where Oscar kept his keys, the umbrella stand, and the collection of sneakers and flip-flops lined up against the wall.

I focused my seer sight on everything. Nothing Otherworldly here. I raised my voice. "Oscar?"

Crickets.

I went through the rest of the house room by room with Zach hot on my heels, his nails clicking on the hardwood floors. The living room—mismatched sofa and recliner and coffee table with the big TV at the far end of the room. The kitchen, where a single glass of whisky sat half-drunk on the breakfast table. Oscar would never have left it like that. *Waste of good,* he'd have said.

A close look told me the whisky hadn't been magicked or poisoned. Nothing there but single malt. I downed it in one burning swallow that warmed my chest and let me breathe a little slower. Other than that, it didn't help at all. It didn't undo what Melody had done or bring Oscar running.

I checked the rest of the house. Bathroom: nothing. Ditto the bedroom. And then there was the study, which was all wrong. Not magically wrong. Something else.

Not the furniture—it still held a big, maple desk, a thick, brown rug, a brown leather sofa, and floor-to-ceiling bookcases that spanned the entire room. Any other time I'd been in there, hundreds of times over the years, Oscar's desk had been littered with layers of books. Grimoires. Books of Shadows. History and folklore. Everything magical or with the potential to help him decode magic. Regardless of whether something specifically bad was going down, he always wanted to learn the next thing. You never knew when it might come in handy to stop a bad guy or save your life. That was the code he lived by. The one he taught me to live by, too.

And now? The desk was spotless. Not a single book. Not even a speck of dust. Every volume had been re-shelved.

I made my way to the nearest bookcase. Stopped halfway there when I heard a thud— Zach had hopped onto the sofa. Wet dog on leather. Oscar would be pissed.

One problem at a time.

The books had been put back in no logical order that I could make out, and I ought to know. He'd made me organize them when I first started working with him. Said it'd be a good idea for me to get familiar as soon as possible. If he'd put the books back all willy-nilly, he'd been in a hurry. Or he'd wanted to make it harder for unwanted visitors to find stuff.

That second thought would never have occurred to me on your basic day. Oscar didn't have unwanted visitors. No one got in unless he invited them. If they tried, the house would cherry pick from their brains the thing they feared most and show it to them in full color, 3D, surround sound.

The only people who ever needed to find books in here? Oscar. Me. My buddy, Kevin. Oscar wouldn't have arranged things to make it harder for any of us. So he had to have been in a hurry.

I told myself that. But I didn't believe it. I believed the other thing down to the marrow of my bones without any reason.

Which meant it had to be true. Seer's intuition.

Oscar had said I'd develop that sooner or later, and that I wouldn't have control over it until I faced my demons. I'd been all psyched that I'd know when my Chem teacher would throw pop quizzes. It never occurred to me that my first intuition would happen like this.

Once the intuition came, other stuff would follow. Like the ability to have visions. Not just of the future, but of the past. Of the present—what other people were doing across town or on the other side of the world or in the Faery realm.

That was a lot of power. A lot of responsibility.

Think.

Who did Oscar fear would get in? What was he afraid they'd find in the books? Had they been here already? Had they done something to Oscar?

No answer from my newfound intuition.

I shook my head to clear it. Turned around and studied the desk one more time.

Laptop and printer off. Notepad, pens, and pencils stacked neatly in the corner. Sea glass paperweight holding down a stack of bills. I thumbed through them with not inconsiderable pain. All I found was that the electric this month would be a ball-buster.

I searched the drawers. Found files, a pack of peppermint gum, a cigar wrapped in plastic, a box of matches. And Oscar's journal.

I read the last couple of pages, or tried to—the dude had nearly illegible handwriting. At this point, I caught about three-fourths of what he tried to say.

There had been portents. Signs of something super bad on the horizon. Starting with an entire murder of crows perched in the oak outside about two weeks ago. Around the time Melody said she'd melted the wheel of that car.

Since then, there'd been water on his stovetop that boiled without a fire under it, two fender-benders in the Honda, and a red sunset. He mentioned the portal outside the pub and the info that nefarious characters would be coming through tonight. The end.

I stuck the journal into the waistband of my shorts. I didn't want the thing out of my sight. If I left it in this room while I went to look someplace else, it might not be there when I got back. Despite the fact that the house was empty except for a dog and me. Again, no reason for that except that my world—for all I knew, the whole world—had gone to hell in the proverbial hand basket and my eyes were black and Oscar was missing and everything was w.r.o.n.g.

I looked at the books again. Meticulously, from the top of the first shelf all the way to the bottom of the last. I didn't see anything Oscar would've had a reason to hide. I considered taking it all apart, but I had no idea what to look for. And I didn't want to undo any kind of magic he'd used to conceal.

There was nothing else I could do here. I had Oscar's journal. I could figure this out. I had to.

I whistled at Zach.

His ears perked up. He watched me until I got to the office door, then hurried after me to the bathroom.

I fumbled through the medicine cabinet until I found what I was looking for. Oscar had fried his palms on a mission three months ago. He wouldn't tell me what'd happened. Where he'd gone or whom he'd gone up against. I only knew he'd come home and headed straight for urgent care, where they'd set him up with a special ointment for the burns and a whole lot of sterile gauze and tape.

By the time I finished fooling with it all, I had what appeared to be ten miniature mummies on most of my fingertips. If I looked ridiculous, so what? Who was I going to impress? The dog?

I led Zach back to the front door, re-scanning the living room from the corner of my eye. And froze. The TV. There might be something about what had happened on TV.

I found the remote on the coffee table and perched on the edge of the recliner while the cable kicked in and the big screen came to life. Oscar had the thing tuned to one of the networks. Probably he'd been watching the local news. Now? Nothing but snow.

I flipped through channel after channel. Nothing.

I pulled out my phone. Tried the 'net. I couldn't get to it. Not to any of my social networks. Not even to a search engine. I had no bars and a message at the top of the screen that read No Service.

No Internet. No phone. Weird, since the electricity still worked. I guess there was no accounting for magic.

Still, that backed up my worry that whatever had happened hadn't just happened to the city, but the world.

How could one girl have done all that?

What had happened to all those people outside the bar? The people in the cars? Where had everyone gone? Was *everyone* gone? My friends? My family?

I flew out of the chair and outside so fast I almost forgot to close the door behind me. I fumbled the key, but managed to get the lock turned. As fast as I could, I buckled the dog into the passenger seat and drove the half mile to my house like a combination NASCAR-obstacle course champion.

I ran every light. No one stopped me. There was no one else on the road. Zach barked all the way there and up the long driveway that ended in the shadow of my parents' two-story McMansion.

Two Range Rovers in the garage. So they had to be home.

Zach followed me through the backyard gate, through the wet grass grown up over the stepping stones, and through the glass French doors that opened into the kitchen. We tracked mud on the tile.

The clock above the stove ticked away a minute. The night light near the sink glowed gently over an empty water glass, still wet from a middle-of-the-night sip. The refrigerator's motor kicked in, dialing up my already frayed nerves.

I took the stairs two at a time, making all kinds of thump-and-squeak noise. Zach climbed hot on my heels. We ran down the hall, past the guest room and my room. The door to my parents' room rested half-open.

They were light sleepers. One of them ought to have turned on a lamp and sat up in bed by now. But no one had.

I pushed the door open all the way and stepped inside. Two shapes lay under the covers, one on his back and the other curled on her side, a tuft of auburn hair sticking up. How they always slept. I breathed in the familiar scent of vanilla potpourri, Mom's favorite. The dog nuzzled the backs of my knees.

I walked over to the bed and knelt. Shook Mom's shoulder. No response. I leaned down near her face and felt her breath on my cheek. I shook her harder. No effect.

Nausea bloomed in the pit of my belly. "Mom?"

Nothing.

"Mom!"

She slept on as if I wasn't in the room at all. Like I didn't even exist.

I tried Dad. He was also alive, but wouldn't wake, either.

Something was very wrong. Not people-disappeared-while-driving-their-cars wrong, but bad. Worse. These were my *parents*. Was their super sleep magical? Or medical?

And how come I found my parents in their own bed when so many people had just up and disappeared?

Goddamn magic.

I made myself take slow, methodical breaths and looked at my folks with every ounce of my seer's eyes. Their edges glowed. It was faint, but it was there. They might still be in the world, but they'd changed somehow. Whatever Melody had done, she'd done it to them, too.

I backed out of there on shaking legs and kept going all the way to my own room. The backs of my knees hit the edge of the bed and I went down in a heap on the floor, burying my face in my hands.

Mom and Dad wouldn't wake up. Mom and Dad in some kind of demon-induced sleep. Would they stay that way forever? Was there some kind of spell I could do to put them back they way they ought to be?

I didn't know any spells that could do that. My stuff was super specific. How to get Otherworlders to go home. How to blunt bad magic. How to see things.

Oscar would know what to do. A full seer like him would have a lot more tricks up his sleeve. But Oscar had gone away. Or he'd been taken. Or demon-magicked away. He wasn't there to ask. Or to help. Or to anything.

I was on my own.

Zach nuzzled the top of my head. So, correction, the dog and me, we were on our own for now.

I had friends—four of them, plus other assorted freaks—who might be in the same sitch as my parents. Or disappeared like Oscar and the people who vanished from their cars and the sidewalks and the streets. I had to know. And I couldn't call or text. I had to find them the old-fashioned way. Going to their houses or otherwise tracking them down. Starting with my best friend.

Which meant getting up and getting out. I had second thoughts about leaving my parents, but I couldn't do anything for them here. Not yet. So I wiped my eyes and looked up and got an eyeful of my desk with its docking station for my tunes and my laptop, my backpack full of books on the chair. Walls plastered with a mix of Houston Texans posters and folk art related to my seer gig. And one wet dog that I'd be taking with me. Couldn't leave him alone in a strange place. Besides, he was the only normal I'd seen since the world went to hell.

I pushed to my feet, walked into the bathroom, and gazed into the mirror. My eyes? Still black. My face had an energy around it that looked a lot like Melody's. Muddy and brimming with no good.

Had she rubbed off on me? Like, just by touching me? Had her magic done this? What did it mean? What did everything mean?

I had to find my friends. I had to figure out what exactly had happened. What Melody did. How to fix it.

Think, dude. Think.

My parents. The state of Oscar's library. My black eyes. All the people who'd vanished from their cars and from the sidewalks and the streets. All of them clues.

Plus one more, very large and important clue. The tattoo on Melody's back. It'd moved on her skin.

I knew one person—and one person only—who could create ink like that.

CHAPTER 3

I PARKED THE Explorer at the curb in front of Snake Bite Tattoo as the rising sun flooded the street with first light. Zach took one look at the place and whined, but he followed me onto the street and stayed by my side. At least it'd stopped raining.

This neighborhood ought to have been shut down so early in the morning. Quiet and peaceful. But heavy metal poured from the open door of the leather bar across the street, where nobody appeared to be partying but where everybody had left their Harleys and Hondas in the lot. On my side of the road, a guy with a half-empty bottle of whisky in his hand slept propped against front wall of the building. He muttered to himself, maybe talking to somebody in his dreams. But he didn't look anything other than asleep, thank God.

A couple of crows landed on the roof in front of me. They looked at me with intelligent eyes. Crazy spooky. One of them flapped its wings. I jumped like a scared child.

A CLOSED sign hung in the Snake Bite's burglar-barred window, the lights in the front room dim, but not dark. I banged on the glass. Glimpsed a shadow move in the back.

"Malek!" I yelled.

The drunk, sleeping guy stirred for a second, then settled down.

A face flashed on the other side of the shop window, pale and pissed. A beat later, the door opened.

Malek narrowed his gray eyes the minute he glanced at mine. He wore his traditional uniform: pristine, white tank and a pair of black jeans with black combat boots. His bald head gleamed, even in the dark. His mouth, blood red inside the frame of a dark goatee.

He was a god. *The* tempter. As in the serpent from the Garden of Eden. Crazy, right? But I'd met the dude once before and he scared the shit out of me. Not because he did anything. Just from proximity.

Oscar said he'd tempted one too many humans and been punished for it. He'd lost his silver tongue. Actually, he'd lost the ability to speak at all. Which was why when he had something to say, he raised his hands to sign. Like now.

Where the hell have you been?

All the hairs on my arms stood at attention. I wondered if he'd been to Hell, whether he'd liked it.

"Traffic. Abandoned cars everywhere. Oscar's missing. Lots of people are missing."

One corner of Malek's mouth curved. *Who's the mutt?*

"Found him."

And your fingers?

"Long story."

Malek stepped back from the door and let us in.

Even in the dark, the floor looked eat-off-of-it clean. The coffee table held a perfect fan of tat magazines. Normal for Snake Bite. The unusual? A gun rested on the front counter next to the cheap jewelry for piercings and a rack of comics.

"Who're you planning to shoot?" I asked.

Maybe him. Malek cocked his head at the vinyl sofa by the window.

Someone had been stretched out on it, and I hadn't been able to see them from outside. Now they—a guy, by the shape—sat up and swung his legs front and center. The way he stood up, he looked familiar. Way too big around the shoulders, but still.

I blew out a breath I hadn't realized I'd been holding. Relief shook me to my core.

"Kevin?"

"Mostly," he said.

"What's that mean?"

He stepped out of the shadows.

He had on the same T-shirt, jeans, and sneakers he always wore, but he also had on a jean jacket, and it was summer-hot outside, and he had brand new, linebacker-wide shoulders. His brown hair hung extra-shaggy to his shoulders. Something white poked out. Really thin and almost translucent. Something feather-shaped.

"Tell me that's not what I think it is," I said.

"Sorry, man."

"Tell me."

"Showing's better."

Kevin slipped off his jacket and T-shirt, showing off his study-too-much, work-out-too-little physique. That was the normal. The extremely abnormal was the pair of white, finely feathered wings growing from his shoulder blades.

My mouth fell open. "What?"

"Faery wings. Can you believe this?"

It made a kind of weird sense. Kev had just been some guy until magic had awakened in him, giving him the power to hear thoughts when danger rose.

Then the Faery King had come for him. Kev had taken every risk to get free, to save his dad and the rest of us. He feared one thing and one thing only—losing his humanity. He had solid reasons to be afraid of that. He lived in both worlds, a go-between humans and fae. And he'd seen it happen to someone he cared about.

He took a deep breath and spoke in a rush. "I was down at the bus again last night, looking for the Singer."

The Singer. I introduced Kevin to her. Once upon a time, she'd been a human girl who'd fronted a rock band, a girl with an unearthly voice that made people feel what she wanted them to feel. When she sang, she tapped into pure, raw emotion. Her connection with her fans was magical.

The Faery King decided he needed her talent at his disposal, so he marked her with his magic and, slowly but surely, she began to change. She grew translucent wings and her eyes turned from blue to violet and the power in her voice became undeniable.

When she couldn't hide her transformation anymore, she left home and went to live in the bus with her oil paintings and a bottomless bottle of patchouli. She still sang from time to time, the kinds of shows where people literally laughed or cried or jumped each other's bones right then and there.

She fell hard for Kev. Like, love at first sight. She gave up the remnants of her humanity to help him.

After that, she belonged to the Faery King. She'd vanished from our world. She was lost. Kev was determined to find her. Some of that was because of what she'd done for him, and some of it was because he'd fallen just as hard for her. Problematic, because he had a girlfriend whom he also loved. A no-win situation. Someone was going to get hurt. I worried about that.

I worried about my friend.

I'd tried to tell him there was no use looking for the Singer, that she'd let him know when she wanted to be found. Still, he'd gone to the bus almost every night. He'd traveled into Faery, searching. Nothing had worked.

"And?" I asked.

He looked at me, eyes wide. "She was there."

Relief roared through me. She'd know what to do. She'd help us. Wouldn't she? But why was she back now, all of a sudden? And where was she? Why hadn't she come with Kev?

On the heels of that, another question floated to the top of my thoughts: why hadn't I known immediately that the Singer had entered the city? It was my job to know. Lives depended on it.

"I pinched myself," Kev said. "I thought maybe I was hallucinating. That she couldn't be real. She refused to tell me where she's been all this time. She just said she was here now because something terrible was about to happen."

Just like the fae cops.

"All of a sudden the world went pear-shaped. We passed out, both of us. And when we woke up, I was like this. The Singer took one look at me, booted me out of the bus, and sent me here. Then the bus disappeared in a flash." Kevin snapped his fingers. "She took it back to Faery, man. She had the most frightened look on her face. Like she'd seen a ghost."

He shrugged. Or I thought he did. Hard to tell with those wings. "Did she say anything about your shiny, new appendages before she kicked you out?"

"Not specifically. She said something like this happened before. That the borders would have to be sealed. They couldn't risk the realm becoming contaminated. I asked her what she meant. She just told me to come here and wait for you. How do you know this bald-headed, not human, I-don't-know-what-the-hell-he-is? No offense, man, but this place gives me the hardcore creeps."

Malek grinned. The sight of it scraped my brain like fingernails on a chalkboard.

I chose my words carefully. "He's a friend of a friend."

"I don't understand anything he says."

"You need a crash course in American Sign Language, dude."

"The Singer didn't mention that. She just said you'd be coming here, Rude. She said you'd know what to do."

"Really?"

"You don't know anything, do you?"

"Working on it." I turned to Malek. "You do a tattoo lately on a girl's back? A full back piece?"

I've done seven, Malek signed.

"This girl's name is Melody. She goes to our school. Blond, blue eyes, worry line in her forehead. Please tell me you remember her."

Yeah. What about her?

"She started all this."

Kevin shook his head. "You're kidding. Melody?"

"Afraid so."

"How?"

"She's part demon."

"How did we not know that? We see her every day in class. In the halls."

"It's kind of new. With the manifesting, anyway. Malek, what did you ink on her?"

He studied us a minute. Then he waved for us to follow him into the back. The overhead lights seemed extra bright after the dimness up front. It took a second for my eyes to adjust, and even then, they felt as if someone had taken a branding iron to them.

The room smelled of disinfectant. Photos of tribal tattoos covered all the walls, floor to ceiling. The chair and table where Malek did most of his work had been wiped clean, not just of germs but of magical traces, too. The counter held a capped assortment of colored inks, clean and prepped tattoo guns, ointment, and paper towels. An old school stereo system took up the rest of the counter space.

I punched the ON button. *Disturbed* blared at deafening decibels. I shut it off fast. The bass echoed in my ears. Malek glanced at me over his shoulder. Kevin and the dog stared at me.

"Sorry," I said.

Kevin peered at me. "What's up with your eyes?"

"Wish I knew. It's freaking me out."

Malek pulled a piece of paper from the files. And a blank notebook and pen. He placed it all on top of the work table. *This is the drawing I did for that girl.*

The city skyline. Downtown Houston in all its glory, lit up like at Christmas with red and green lights reflecting off glass and steel. Life-like and real in every way.

"Not exactly hearts and butterflies," Kevin said.

He wrote for Kev's benefit. *Don't do those.*

"What kind of magic did you put into this?" I asked.

Same as for all of them.

Kevin looked at him, then at me. Raised a brow.

"His blood," I said. "He infuses the ink with it."

"Gross."

Malek smirked.

"What did she ask for?"

A place to call home. Said she'd never felt like she had one. She was living somewhere new, and she wanted to start over. To be who her heart told her she was. She didn't have the power to make a fresh beginning, but I could help her with that.

"The rumors from school?" Kev asked. "Her dad, getting kicked out?

"True," I said. "She told me before she turned the world upside down. She came to me for help."

Nice job, Malek wrote.

The sarcasm stung. A wave of anger surged through me. I swallowed it and filled them in. Afterward, Kev stared and Malek furrowed his brow.

"What was so special about the spell you inked on Melody's back?" I asked. "I mean, was it something besides a new home? Because even if she is part demon, even if she's having power surges because she can't control what she's doing, she shouldn't have been able to make people disappear or change them. She shouldn't have been able to cut off communication, either. Phones not working. No Internet. There has to be something else going on here.

"She was talking about melting a trash can. A steering wheel. We're a long ways from that here, don't you think?"

Malek nodded. *I didn't give her control over the city, if that's what you're thinking. I gave her the power to remake her life.*

"It doesn't make sense, dude." A place to call home. A fresh start. The power to remake her life. "The city's not her life."

Malek smoothed his goatee with one hand, the other resting on the drawing.

"Think of something?" I asked.

It's possible that my magic connected her life to the city. It's not what I meant to do.

Unbelievable. "You're saying you possibly screwed up here?"

I'm saying I can't be sure.

"Find a way."

He met my gaze. His eyes looked older than God. *I need to see her again.*

Kev leaned forward, elbows on the table. "You can't just reach out to her? She carries your magic. You're connected."

I sever those ties with my clients once the job is done.

"How?" Kevin asked. "Why?"

Malek signed to me. *He really doesn't know?*

I shook my head.

Malek went back to the notepad. *The people who come to me are broken. They pay a terrible price for the work I do, and they don't always like the results. A mother whose child is missing wants to know what happened to her little girl. I give her an answer so she can find the child. Bury her. Not a happy ending. A man whose wife was dying of cancer asked for her to be healed. I warned him. He was still surprised when the cancer that had nearly eaten her alive ended up inside him. She lived. He died a horrible death. Why would I want to be connected to any of that? Once a job is done, it's done.*

Kev's mouth fell open.

Malek wasn't human. He'd never been human. He didn't have human morality. His ethics came from a different experience. Kevin needed a touchstone to understand.

"He's like the King," I said.

The expression in Kev's eyes went flat. The King had hurt his father. Hurt the Singer. Changed Kev's life forever. "What did those people pay for the honor of wearing your work?"

Malek cocked his head at Kevin in a way that made me worry. I laid a hand on Kev's arm.

Malek saw, of course. He wrote on the notepad. *I won't hurt him. Being stupid's not a crime.*

Which only made Kevin angrier. I wrapped my fingers around his arm and squeezed.

The woman I mentioned gave me her life savings. The man who died of cancer gave me his soul. Does it make you feel better to know?

Kevin's voice failed him. His question came out a whisper. "His soul?"

That was the price for his wish. If you ever come to me for a tattoo, be sure you're willing to pay what it costs.

"That'll never happen."

Never say never.

I let go of Kev's arm and changed the subject. "Malek, what did Melody pay?"

Most of her new life. She got ten years to live, and I got the rest of her years.

"Which means she'd live to be twenty-eight?" I asked.

Malek nodded.

Ten years. Seemed like a lot until you thought about the fact that average lifespan would've gotten her to seventy or eighty. "Who would be stupid enough to take that deal?"

A desperate girl.

"Who you took advantage of," Kevin said.

Clearly, she took advantage of me.

"Clearly, this whole thing is fucked up beyond belief," I said. "What can we do to reverse it?"

Find her. You know how to track a demon?

"Half-demon."

Whatever. You know how?

"I know a little about Melody. About her life. We need someone who knows her better, who maybe can tell us the places she'd go to hang out. Or maybe they noticed something different about her from before."

Kevin took his elbows off the table and stood up straight. "Amy. She has more classes with Melody than the rest of us."

Amy, Kevin's girlfriend. The human girl who wanted him more than he wanted her. The girl who could never be as magical as the Singer. Amy should've broken up with him already. She was brilliant and awesome and she deserved better than a boyfriend who went out every night looking for someone else.

If Amy had classes with Melody, that didn't make them friends, but it was a lead. Something we could do. "Is Amy okay?"

"I tried to text her on the way here, but my phone didn't work." He pushed the hair back from his forehead.

Go, Malek wrote. *Let me know what you find out.*

"We'll be back as soon as we can," I said.

If that girl made this mess, I want her dead.

What? "Dead?"

She knew what she was doing when she came to me for the ink. Or if she didn't plan it in advance, she did it on the fly, and that means the kind of power she's got is off the charts. She can't be walking around and breathing with that much juice.

"If she didn't premeditate it, then it was an accident," I said. "You can't hold her responsible for an accident. Not like that."

Your cops and your courts do it all the time.

"Sometimes they get it right and a lot of times they really don't. Too many people who should be in prison aren't, and too many people who have no business being locked up are serving years they shouldn't be. You know that, so don't give me that bullshit. Besides, you're not a cop and you're not a judge."

Let's get something straight here, Rude. This is not your normal, human world we're talking about. This is magical and dangerous. You're the cop here. That's your job. You're the faery seer.

"Apprentice," I said.

No. You were an apprentice yesterday. It doesn't matter whether you're done with your training. Oscar's gone and you're all we've got in the faery seer department, so man up. Do what needs to be done.

It mattered to me. I still had a couple of years to go under Oscar before I got promoted. Or graduated. Whatever. I wasn't ready. I didn't have all the knowledge I'd need to go up against someone like Melody. If I needed to go up against her at all.

I couldn't ignore the possibility that she'd tricked Malek. It could've gone down like that. But I didn't believe it. She was the same age as Kevin and me. She'd had a hard life and she wanted a new beginning and why would she screw it up so royally if she could help it? Who would do something like that?

If we could find her, we could talk to her. Find out what happened and make it right. Maybe I wouldn't need to know everything. Maybe I could skate by on the training I already had.

"She came to me for help, Malek."

So help her. Kill her. If she's as innocent as you think she is, she'll thank you.

"No." I didn't care whether Malek was a god, whether he could take me out with a flick of his finger. I would not kill for him.

If you want my help—and you're going to need it, make no mistake—you'll do it. And you'll swear to do it.

Kevin looked from Malek's words on the paper to me. "He's serious?"

"Deadly."

I couldn't promise to kill Melody. I wouldn't. But if things did go bad for any reason, we might need Malek's help. If I didn't agree to his terms now, we might be kissing our asses goodbye, much less any chance of fixing this horrible mess.

"Here's my counteroffer," I said. "I'll swear to do justice."

Malek studied me. *Whatever that turns out to be?*

"Yes."

He reached out a hand for me to shake. I took it. Felt a pinprick of pain. Pulled back my hand to see a tiny red dot in the center of my palm.

My blood. "You cut me?"

It's called a blood oath. Don't try to weasel out.

"And now you're calling me a liar?"

I don't know yet. I don't know you, introductions from Oscar aside. I trust actions, not words. Show me who you are.

My hands curled into fists.

Don't try to back out of your promise. The consequences will be severe. Now get to work.

Kevin started to say something. I gave him my best *shut up right the hell now* look and thought at him, too. He snapped his mouth closed.

Malek herded us out and bolted the door behind us.

A breeze brought us the stench of the dumpster around the corner. The sun had finished rising, and lit all the post-apocalyptic ugliness of the street with its strong glow. The leather bar, where the tunes still played. The abandoned cars I'd pushed to the sides of the street or slalomed around. The empty Scotch bottle pushed by into the curb by the wind.

I could've sworn that bottle had been cupped in the hand of the passed-out drunk on the sidewalk. I turned to look. The passed-out drunk was gone.

"The hell?" Kev punched me in the arm. "Some friend of a friend."

"I may have exaggerated."

I filled him in about Malek, listening to the words as they rolled off my tongue with mounting horror. What Malek was. How he'd ended up tongue-tied. And the rest? No way to sugar coat it. "Look, dude, the last person to double-cross the guy ended up beaten to death in an alley. And the time before that, some dude tried to save his dying girlfriend's life by knocking Malek out and draining some of his blood so the girl could drink it. I mean, a god's blood, right? Powerful stuff. The girl died screaming before she bled out through her eyes and ears and mouth, and Malek killed the boyfriend."

"Jesus H. Christ in a sidecar."

"Yeah. I came here because of Melody. Because of the ink on her back. Not because Malek is my buddy."

"This is so fucked up, Rude."

I laced my fingers on top of my head, pressing down hard, hoping the sensation would help me focus.

"You told Malek no. You negotiated with a god. You made him a promise and if you don't keep it, he'll—"

"I know, Kev."

"How could you do all that? You didn't even beak a sweat. Who are you, man?"

He looked at me as if I was some kind of alien, not the guy he knew from school. Not the friend who'd stuck by him when practically no one else had.

I knew everyone, and everyone thought they knew me, but they didn't. I couldn't let them. Kev was one of the chosen few who understood the danger I dealt with. I thought he'd get it.

"Never show fear," I said.

"Even if you're terrified?"

"Especially then. It makes them think you're weak and it can get you killed."

Kevin stared at me. "How're you supposed to get justice, Rude?"

"I don't know. I only know that if I dish it out, I have to take mine, too. If I'm dirty, that could be bad. That's what worries me there."

"You're not, though. Bad, that is."

It was entirely possible I'd done something wrong enough to get me in trouble without even knowing it. Or that I did it and then pushed it out of my mind. I was basically a good person. I wanted to be. And that made selective memory pretty attractive. I'd learned that from Oscar. Even if he'd disappeared from the scene, and even if Malek seemed to think I'd received a battlefield promotion to full seer, I was still Oscar's student. Lessons mattered.

"Time will tell." If I didn't lose my life or my mind first. If I could hold it together long enough to help everyone else.

Kev sighed. He contracted his wings clumsily until they lay as flat against his back as he could manage, then slipped on his T-shirt and jacket.

"It's too hot for that, dude."

"I can deal with it—the whole wings thing. Okay, maybe I can't exactly deal, but I know Amy won't be able to, and I don't want her to see me this way until I have a chance to explain first."

I didn't think any explanation would make things better, but that wasn't up to me. I changed the subject. "Where's your bike? You rode from downtown, right?"

He pointed to the closest signpost. No Parking This Side of the Street Mon. through Fri. 6:00 AM to 6:00 PM. He'd chained his bike to it. I opened the back of the Explorer while he unlocked it. It fit just fine without me having to lay down the rear seats.

Zach didn't appreciate being pushed to the back seat. He leaned forward far enough to rest his head on my shoulder while I started the car. Before I could put my foot on the gas, intuition socked me in the back of the head. I froze.

"What's up?"

"Your wings. You're the go-between for humans and fae, dude. You have faery wings, but you're not fae. You're still you."

"That's just it, Rude. I don't feel entirely human."

"A hybrid, maybe?"

"You're saying that I look like what I do?"

"No, not what you do. What you *are*, dude."

He drummed his fingers on the armrest. "And your eyes?"

"I'm a faery seer apprentice. I see things that would freak the hell out of people. Dark things. My parents are the opposite. They don't see anything at all, at least not about me. It's like I'm not even there half the time. Maybe the part of them that should be, you know, parents, is asleep."

Or maybe I'd put them to sleep.

I shook my head hard, and the thought disintegrated, thank all the powers. But the aftertaste of it stuck around to muck up my mouth.

"That's some theory," Kev said.

I focused on what he'd said. On him. "It's what we've got. Unless you can think of a better explanation."

"I got nothing." He rubbed his eyes. "Amy's house. Then we get a hold of everyone else. We get the gang together. Make sure everybody's all right. Scott. Stacy. Mr. Nance."

Kevin's entirely normal buddy, our resident Witch, and the Singer's father, who happened to be the school counselor. "Plus your dad."

"Shit." He pulled out his phone.

"That's not gonna work."

He tried anyway. Then he pitched the phone into the change tray below the dash.

"We could split up," he said. "Cover more ground."

Tempting. But when I imagined us going our separate ways to save time, I felt like I could throw up. Seer's intuition again. "No. That gives me big, bad feelings."

He met my gaze. "Okay, but we have to hurry."

"Agreed. Amy's—you worried about what we're gonna find there?"

"I'm worried about what we're gonna find everywhere. I'm trying not to."

If Amy hadn't gone poof like most of the people in the city, she might not be the Amy we knew when we found her. She was a normal girl, except she dated Kevin, and she spent a lot of her time with me.

She never really felt she belonged.

Kind of like Melody.

CHAPTER 4

AMY'S HOUSE SAT quiet—too quiet—on a corner lot on the other side of the freeway from where Kev and I lived. The downstairs windows, dark and blank like dead eyes. One light on upstairs. And one light on in the attic. Tall pines in the front yard drank in the sunlight. A couple of squirrels foraged in their shadows.

In spite of that temptation, Zach refused to get out of the car. I cracked the windows and left him inside. When we stepped away from the car, he whined.

The hairs on the back of my neck rose. I checked the street. Watched for anything out of the ordinary. Except everything was out of the ordinary. Empty. So why did standing on the porch surrounded by potted plants and wind chimes tinkling in the breeze make me feel like a target?

I stood behind Kevin while he knocked on the front door. No one came. He tried again. Fidgeted and wiped his palms on his jeans.

"You have a key?" I asked.

He shook his head. "Break it down? I have to know if she's in there. If she's okay."

I could try to pick the lock, but I didn't have a ton of skill in that area. We could go through a window. Or...I reached over and tried the knob. It turned, lock-free. The door swung open.

Kevin glanced at me over his shoulder. Stepped inside.

A note had been duct-taped to the wall in the entry. One word, all caps, written in red lipstick. Shhhh!

Kevin sucked in a breath.

I slipped by him and took a look around on the first floor while he headed up the stairs. Coffee maker on, thin film of burnt nasty in the bottom of the glass carafe—I flipped off the power switch. TV on, showing nothing but snow, just like Oscar's. Master bedroom, empty.

Upstairs, a long hall led to Amy's room. Her door was closed. Kev knelt a few feet away, sorting through a pile of twigs that'd been swept against the baseboard.

No, not twigs. Bones. Small ones. Like from an animal.

Amy had two cats and I hadn't seen either of them yet.

I shivered and glanced up. The door to attic had been rigged with a string wrapped around the neck of an empty glass soda bottle. If the door came down, that bottle would smash against something—the back of door itself. Or the nearest wall. An early warning system?

Kev rose and stepped around me, opening Amy's door. The hinges had been oiled—the viscous stuff literally dripped from the metal. Sunlight flooded the hall. Dust motes floated in the air.

The bed had either been made pathologically early or it hadn't been slept in. Amy's unopened backpack sat on the desk chair. Tiny pots of purple, yellow, and green cacti lined the windowsill. The shaggy red rug had been rolled up, glass from a busted light bulb spread on the hardwood floor in front of the walk-in closet. Closed door again.

All the clothes had been pulled off their hangers and piled into a heap in the farthest corner.

Amy was under them, dressed in a pink T-shirt, black jeans, and boots like Malek's. She'd pulled her knees pulled to her chest. Her whole body shook. Eyes closed. Headset covering her ears. Her long blue-black hair hid half of her face.

Kevin wrapped her in his arms.

That only made the trembling worse. She pressed her whole self into Kev's chest. He opened his mouth to say something.

She clamped a hand over his lips.

Kev helped her unfurl and stand. Her legs didn't want to hold her, so she leaned against him. Her face was pale, no color in her cheeks. Even her eyes looked as if they'd been bleached.

Out, I mouthed.

Kevin nodded. After a second, so did Amy. She pointed to her pack on the chair. I slung it over my shoulder.

I thought she might say something as soon as we were out of the house. She cocked her head toward the Explorer.

Kev slid into the back seat with her. Zach jumped up front.

I turned around in the driver's seat so I could see her clearly. She shook her head. Looked at the ignition. So I turned the key. And I drove. Turned the wheel in the right direction to get us to a hospital. The girl was in capital-S shock.

Shock was a good word to describe everything. The world had turned upside down, and I hadn't seen a single cop or fire truck or ambulance. What would the hospital be like? Would there even be any doctors there? Or would they have disappeared like nearly everyone else?

Amy spoke a single word. Her voice shook so bad, she could barely get it out. "Okay."

"Okay what?" I asked.

"Stop the car."

I pulled over. Turned around again.

Kevin brushed the hair from her eyes. "There's blood on your shirt. Please tell me it's not yours."

Blood? I hadn't noticed. How could I not have noticed? "Are you hurt?"

Amy leaned forward. Dug her nails into my headrest. "Hurt doesn't even begin to describe it."

"Whose blood?" Kev asked.

"Some of it's my mom's. Blink scratched her."

Blink the tabby cat. The one who spent all his time looking out the windows. "Why?"

"He didn't want to be eaten. Too bad for him, right?"

"The bones in the hall?" I asked.

She wiped at her eyes.

Kevin sucked in a breath. "Both of them?"

She spat the words out in a rush. "It started last night. In the middle of the night. Mom screamed and I bolted out of bed and ran to see what'd happened. That's when I saw her with Blink. She looked out of her mind. She had to be out of her mind. What she did—what they both did, her and Dad. Then they went up into the attic. Dad—he said there were birds up there. Nesting birds and squirrels and he was drooling when he said it, Rude. I slammed the door behind them. I thought they'd come down. Come after me."

"So you booby trapped the door," I said.

"Stupid, huh?"

"No." Kevin took her hands in his. "But why didn't you get out of there?"

"I tried to call you," she said. "No signal on my cell. And the house phone didn't work."

"I would've come."

"I know. I thought about going to your house."

Kevin wouldn't have been there. I didn't feel compelled to say that. Neither did he.

"Why didn't you?" he asked.

"You mean why did I hide in the closet like a five-year-old?"

"No. Yes."

"I was afraid of running into crazy on the way there. Afraid if your dad answered the door, he'd act like mine. Or that I'd start acting like that."

"So you hid in the closet and waited for it to start?" Kev asked.

She didn't answer. She didn't have to.

"You knew I would come," he said.

She said nothing.

"You knew, right?"

She looked at him. Pasted on a smile that didn't reach her eyes. "Sure."

He shook his head.

"Really," she said.

He matched her grin. Then added a dose of *I believe you* to his expression. She breathed out. Her shoulders dropped. "What's going on?"

I filled her in, from the minute Melody walked up to me outside the pub to the minute we found her. Every detail, down to my eyes and my working theory about why they'd turned all-pupil and black. Kevin's wings weren't mine to tell about, so I waited for him to say something.

He opened his mouth. And closed it again.

Amy didn't notice. She seemed to pull herself together a little. She slipped her hands from Kev's. Straightened in her seat. Combed her fingers through her hair. We had a problem to solve, and Amy had proved she could be counted on to help in a crisis. She'd done it before. She'd do it again.

"We need a plan," she said.

"Besides flying by the seat of my pants?" I asked.

"Your pants are not enough."

Kevin nodded. "I need to check on my dad."

"We," I said. "We stick together, remember?"

Amy pulled her hair back and tied it in a knot. "And Stacy and Scott. Mr. Nance at school. And as much as I hate to say it—because you know I hate her guts with a fiery passion of hate—the Singer."

Kevin cleared his throat. "The Singer's okay. For now, anyway."

"You went to see her first? Before you came to me?"

"Not first. You heard Rude. We came here first."

"Then how do you know?"

"I was at the bus when the shit hit the fan."

"And she was there this time?"

He nodded.

"After all this time, she came back? I thought she was gone. I wanted her to be gone."

That was an extraordinary thing to admit out loud. Her cheeks flushed and her face closed up as soon as she realized what she'd said.

I turned face-forward, eyes on the road. I put the car back in gear.

We had to stop three times on the way to Kevin's to move cars. I couldn't help thinking about the motorcycles at the bar across from Snake Bite. Or how absolutely dead we'd be if the three of us tried to drive those things. The learning curve. And the probable lack of, you know, ambulances with EMTs and doctors and nurses in hospitals. Because we would totally spill. And with our luck—at least how it'd played so far—someone would end up with a fractured skull.

'Course, Kevin might get one without hopping on a Harley. I glanced at Amy through the rearview mirror. She'd crossed her arms over her chest. Pulled as far away from Kev as she could, practically plastered herself against the door. She stared out the window the whole way. When we got out of the car at Kevin's, she slammed it so hard the window glass rattled.

With a look, she dared me to say something about that. I kept my mouth shut.

Kevin's place was one of the few one-story frame houses left in the neighborhood. Red with white trim around the windows and the door, all of which were wide open. The breeze blew back the curtains. A cop car had been crookedly parked in the driveway, engine ticking as it cooled.

A blue-green halo of fae magic hovered all around the car.

I gripped the wheel so tightly, my knuckles turned white. "Assholes."

"They're not in the car," Kevin said.

I nodded. "In the house."

"With my dad."

Kev's father had PTSD from his time with the fae. His wife's death, his own poor life choices, and the fae's magic had driven him out of his mind. Nearly killed him. He hated the fae. No way he'd have let Burns and his jerk of a partner into the house willingly.

We piled out of the car, Zach on our heels. Amy fell behind, and Kev and I turned at the same time to see her frozen in place by the cruiser, staring.

"What?" Kev asked.

"Your back. Your shoulders. You're all wrong."

"The magic that changed the city…it changed some of the people, too." He shifted his weight from one foot to the other. "I have wings."

"Like an angel?"

"Not exactly."

"Faery wings."

He nodded.

"Does that make you one of them."

"Not that I know of. I haven't exactly had a chance to ask anyone yet."

Amy rubbed the bridge of her nose. "This whole thing makes my head hurt."

Kevin held out his hand.

Amy shook her head. She didn't want his help. But she started walking. She motioned for us to go ahead and took two steps to our one until she drew close enough to grab on to the hem of his jacket. He blew out a long breath.

I stole a glance at her. Looked her over for—I don't know—bruises or sadness or something that went deeper than the last twenty-four hours of insanity. It was possible that she'd escaped the magic unscathed. After all, Malek seemed unchanged.

But Malek was already a magical being, and I hadn't seen a human yet who hadn't been affected. Then again, I could count on one hand the number of humans I'd seen since it all went down.

I studied her harder. For a second, I thought I saw fraying around her edges. Like she was starting to come undone. A heartbeat later, she looked just like she always had. Like Amy.

She and Kevin stepped inside.

I did the same—and smacked into them because they'd stopped

cold in front of the entry table, which was cluttered with what looked like every sharp knife from the kitchen, along with a cup of water with a rosary dunked in it. Under the table? A lockbox. The kind people sometimes kept guns in.

Mr. Landon had been amassing an arsenal behind the front door.

Kevin's eyebrows shot up.

The deep, rich perfume of coffee wafted from the next room, along with Mr. Landon's voice. "In here."

We stepped into the kitchen to find Kevin's dad leaning against the counter, laser gaze focused on Officers Burns and Reid, who occupied two of the four foam seats at the breakfast table, steaming mugs in front of them.

Mr. Landon wore sweats and a pair of sneakers. Even in workout clothes, he looked like an accountant. And he looked stone cold sober and normal, thank God.

Burns used his foot to push one of the free chairs out from under the table. "Ma'am."

Amy blinked. "I'm not old enough to be a ma'am."

"Seat's yours, all the same."

She shook her head. Belatedly, she said, "No, thanks."

I moved to stand beside Mr. Landon, Zach sat at my feet. "What's going on here?"

Burns met my gaze, his expression flat. "What's it look like? We're here to reacquire you."

"Reacquire?" Seer's magic rose inside of me, a rainbow of color that deepened with every angry breath I took. "You two left me unconscious on a sidewalk at magical ground zero."

"We took your pulse," Reid said. "You had one. We didn't have time to haul you off the concrete and take you someplace for safekeeping, and we couldn't take you with us. You're contaminated."

Contaminated. For a half-second, my vision turned black.

"Like that, right there," Burns said. "You got dosed. We had to report back to the King. No way would we take you into Faery like that."

The Singer had said something to Kev about needing to shut the gates to the Faery Realm, that what had happened here could affect them. "What does Melody's spell have to do with the King?"

Burns looked at Reid, then at me. "This magic—the spell that changed your world? Something like it has been done before, the last time two of the tribes in Faery were at war. A group of humans with a vested interest in the outcome cast a spell to open the way between the human realm and ours. They wanted to join the battle. Bring human weapons into the mix. An 'assault rifles are better than swords' kind of thing. They brought an infection with them. Not like the flu or the plague—may as well have been the freakin' plague for what it did to us. It made some of us insane. Made some of us monsters."

I mulled his story. Faery could be scary enough without war and human meddling and— "Monsters?"

Burns glanced at Reid, who scratched the spot beneath his nose.

"I wouldn't go so far as claiming they were perfectly normal to begin with," Reid deadpanned. "Everyone's got issues."

Reid was serious. Like, an armchair fae psychologist. "What Melody did—did it knock you out like me?"

"No," Reid said. "You're human, so of course you're losing consciousness no matter what kind of magic you've got. We saw the whole thing."

Burns hugged himself. "That girl—"

"Melody," I said.

"She lit up like the fuse on a bottle rocket. Flames. Sparks. The whole nine. Then she went black on the inside. Like one of your old photo negatives."

I shook my head. No idea what that meant.

Burns fished for different words. "Like…a shadow. Then she disappeared, leaving an outline of fire that burned out a heartbeat later."

"Then what?" I asked.

"Then nothing, except for her shoes," Reid said. "They were all that remained."

Who left their shoes behind when they vanished? Faery tale princesses. Melody was definitely not one of those. "Where'd she go?"

"We couldn't see that without following her, and that would've entailed too much risk."

So, they'd reported to the Faery King.

Kevin cleared his throat. "Again, why are you here?"

"The King ordered us to help you," Reid said. "He told us not to return until the problem was solved."

Burns met Kevin's gaze. "Not just us. He sent the Singer back, too. She has orders to work with you until the world's put right again. He sealed the borders of Faery behind us. No one in or out until this is all over."

"Has that ever happened before?" Kev asked. "The King sealing the borders?"

Burns shook his head. "Not in my memory."

"How long's your memory, man?"

"Six hundred seventy-three years. My mother lived almost two thousand years. I never heard her talk about sealing borders or closing gates, and she told me every tale from her childhood and all the stories her parents gave to her."

That made it a huge deal. A one-in-a-million thing.

"When you said monsters before, what exactly did you mean by that?" I asked.

Reid frowned. "Whatever power we had drove us crazy, and by crazy, I mean homicidal, in some cases what you'd call psychopathic. It was worse for the ones with the most magic—the King, the Queen, the ones with the strongest gifts. Horrible things were done. So many died badly. There were...mutations. We couldn't cure the infection. We had to cut it out. You understand what I mean?"

"You killed the monsters."

His tone turned bitter. "Every last one."

"Including the King and Queen?"

"The royals you know are relatively new."

Relatively.

I read the devastation in the lines around his eyes, the trembling in his fingers. My magic flared, and I saw a river of blood in my mind's eye and felt the suffering that lay behind it: heartbreak, grief.

I swallowed hard. "So the King locked everything down to keep that from happening again. Is he sure he did it in time?"

"He acted as quickly as he could," Burns said. "That's all we know."

"And once we get this mess under control, he'll reopen the way."

Burns inclined his head. "Far as we know."

Kevin fidgeted. "So what now, Rude?"

He wasn't the only one looking at me. They all were.

I don't have what it takes.

I looked at each of them, but none of them had spoken those words or planted them in my mind. The thought had come from me, from deep inside of me.

A tremor started at the base of my spine, working its way up. I willed it to stop. It took every ounce of my will before it did.

I waited a beat, until I felt sure my voice would sound solid. "We still need to get the others. And now we need to head downtown to get the Singer, too. And I want to go back to the scene of the crime and check things out again. See if we can find some clues I was too wrecked to notice before. Am I missing anything?"

"What about going to the girl's house?" Burns asked. "There might be clues there as to what happened or why she did what she did."

"She doesn't have a house," Amy said. "That whole thing with her stepfather? Melody's mom took his side. She kicked her own daughter to the curb."

"Over that asshole?" Kevin thinned his lips.

"Yeah," she said. "Melody's staying with a friend."

"Beth," I said.

She nodded.

"I know you didn't want to before," Kevin said, "but we really should split up. We can cover more ground faster. You check near where Melody went nuclear. Burns and Reid here can fetch Stacy, Scott, and Mr. Nance if he wants to come."

Which he might not, given that the Singer avoided him and their last meeting had basically been goodbye. She was his daughter, but she'd changed so much—from one-hundred-percent rebellious human girl to one-hundred-percent fae in service to the King.

I noticed neither Burns nor Reid complained about being volun-told where to go.

"I should get the Singer," Kevin said.

Amy stood up. "And me? Where do I fit in?"

"You're coming with me," he said.

She shook her head. "What good would I be there? I mean, I could hold your hand and claim my territory, but I can't make you mine if you don't want to be. That's up to you, Kev. I want to be useful. You and Rude have magic. So do Stacy and the Singer. Scott and me, we're the only ones who don't. Which makes us liabilities."

I thought about way she'd been in the car, so angry with Kevin. The glimpse I'd gotten of how fragile she was, how close to the edge she teetered. One shove could make her fall. One push could break her.

Careful, Kev.

His gaze darted my way. He'd heard me.

He swallowed hard. "What do you have in mind?"

"I want to look for Melody," she said. "She's my friend."

"She blew up," Burns said.

"That's not what you said. You said she disappeared."

"Same thing."

"No. It makes a difference. It matters. If she vanished, then she's somewhere."

"Maybe not in this world," Kevin said.

Amy's hands fisted at her sides. "Maybe not. But if she is, I stand the best chance of finding her. I could help her."

"That's what we thought," I said.

"I can do it."

She needed someone to believe in her. I did. She didn't need magical powers to talk to Melody, to talk her down. She just needed to be a human being, someone who could put themselves in Melody's shoes and imagine how it felt to struggle. "I know you can."

Kevin nodded. "Just be careful. Please."

"She won't hurt me."

"She hurt Rude."

"She could've melted me like the steering wheel. But she didn't," I said.

"And what about your eyes?"

"Wings," I countered.

"Parents," Amy said. "I think the damage is done. There doesn't have to be more. I need a way to get around. Kevin, can I have your bike?"

"It's in the back of the Explorer," I said.

Mr. Landon's voice shook. "I'll go with you. We can take my car."

The offer was genuine, but the guy had gotten in way over his head before, with the King. He'd made it back home, with whatever sanity he could grab onto, only because Kevin had big enough brass to challenge the King and enough brains and luck to sort of win. Maybe Mr. Landon couldn't handle another trip like this.

"Sincerely, thanks. But I can take care of myself. Besides, someone has to stay here at home base."

Kevin looked at me. "Your intuition rang mad alarm bells about splitting up before."

I tried to summon the bad feeling I'd had, but it wouldn't come. Not even a little bit. "Amy will be all right."

Kev didn't look convinced.

Amy rubbed her palms on her jeans and stepped over to Kevin, kissed him softly. "See you back here later."

"Careful," he said.

"You, too."

"I love you."

She flashed him a lopsided grin and gave him her best *The Empire Strikes Back* answer. "I know."

A few minutes later, we watched her pedal east down the street, hair flowing behind her. The picture window in Kev's living room framed her for half a minute. She glanced over her shoulder at the bunch of us and waved.

"Burns, you need addresses?" I asked.

He shook his head. "We know where all of you live. Where you spend your time."

In any other circumstances, I'd be pissed. "Bring Scott and Stacy back here."

"What if they're not normal?"

"Do it anyway."

"And then?" Reid asked. "What's next?"

"That's what we're gonna find out."

CHAPTER 5

KEVIN AND I DROVE AN OBSTACLE course of side roads in to downtown while the dog panted in the back seat until the Explorer smelled like dog breath and the air inside felt sticky. Rolling down the windows didn't help. The air stank of sulfur and exhaust— what I'd always imagined Hell smelled like. Melody's apocalypse had detonated the glass and steel office towers, shiny, sharp shards coating the streets and sidewalks.

Passing the park with the reflecting pool in front of City Hall, I caught a glimpse of a man and a woman together, standing in the shattered remains of a streetlight. The guy, he looked okay. The woman, though? Half her head was missing. Most of the back half, actually.

Kevin cleared his throat. "I'm not imagining that, am I?"

I couldn't make my voice work.

"What's wrong with her, Rude?"

I shrugged. I never wanted to see anything like that, ever again. I wanted to help her, but how? How could I possibly fix this mess?

I concentrated on getting to the alley on the other side of downtown where we'd find the Singer. We didn't encounter any other disturbing people or things, and I thanked all the powers for small favors.

The alley looked and felt the same as always, a river of asphalt contained by brick-red warehouses on either side, empty bottles and oily, crumpled paper and aluminum cans collected at the seams. The school bus sat on bald tires at the far end, windows lowered, a string of fairy lights sparking like stars inside and a patchouli incense fumigating the air all around. A single crow perched on the hood.

"Third time I've seen those little black birds since all this started," I said.

"They're all over town," Kevin said. "All the time. It's nothing new."

True, but I usually noticed them at certain times of year, and in much smaller numbers. Their cousins, grackles and jays, were much more common around here. Something felt off. Hell, everything felt off.

"I don't like it," I said.

"It doesn't seem to have an opinion about you."

I rolled my eyes.

The Singer opened the door as we got out of the Explorer. She'd dyed her hair an autumn rainbow, the color of every kind of fallen leaf, and it hung in waves that brushed her shoulders. Freckles dusted her nose. Her violet eyes were rimmed in blue.

She wore a peacock-feather halter and black leather pants. Her feet were bare. Her wings snapped out wide to either side of her back, delicate and see-through, with muscle structure and arteries and veins pumping blood. They looked fragile, but I knew better. They were strong, like her.

She grinned at the dog and knelt on the ground, arms wide. Zach ran to her, tail wagging. She wrapped her arms around him and he resisted the hug by licking her face. She didn't stand again until we closed the distance. I pretended not to notice that her eyes were wet and glanced away while she wiped them with her fingertips.

The power of Faery bled from her every word. "About time you two got here."

Just the sound of her voice shook up all my molecules and put them back together again in a different way. A wanting way. A wave of desire rolled through me. I tried to stop it, but might as well have tried to hold back a tsunami. I stared at her. Couldn't tear my gaze away. This was so much worse than the last time I'd seen her, before her transformation.

"Dude," I whispered.

Kev walked past me and up the steps. He wrapped his arms around her in a friendly hug. The way she closed her eyes when he did that told me everything I needed to know. Her feelings for him hadn't changed. And he held on a little too long.

My heart broke—a little bit for myself, because of the spell she'd cast just by speaking and how it affected me, and a lot for Amy.

The Singer pulled away from Kevin slowly. "Your shoulders are rippling."

"Wings," he said.

"Shit."

"I know."

"We have a lot to talk about. This is your show, Rude, and you're not looking so hot." She turned on her heel and went inside.

Kev and I followed. The smoke inside was so thick it made me cough. The dog let out three rapid sneezes.

"Sorry," she said. "It's the only thing that keeps the sulfur stink out. Smells like rot."

"It does."

"What's decomposing?"

"That's the question," I said.

"Sit. Make yourselves at home." She headed for the back of the bus.

Sit? The Singer's oil paintings covered nearly every seat. Freshly tie-dyed skirts and socks laid out to dry took up the rest of available space. Kev and I moved what we could.

"Five bucks says our asses are purple when we get up," I said.

He didn't laugh.

The Singer returned with three bottles of water and an empty plastic bowl. She tossed one to each of us, then opened hers and drank half the bottle in a long swig. She poured the rest into the bowl for Zach.

"Where'd you find him?" she asked.

"Freeway."

"Lucky."

"Yeah. I don't know what would've happened to him if I hadn't come across him."

"I didn't mean he was lucky. You were. Are." She climbed on top of the nearest bench and perched on the seatback.

"He's a special kind of dog?"

"If you haven't figured it out by now, Rude, I have no hope for you."

Sarcasm. And something else underneath it. "What did you mean with that crack about how I look?"

"You've seen your eyes, right?"

I nodded.

"And your skin?"

"What about my skin?"

"It's wrong, and I'm not talking about your burned fingers." She hooked a thumb over her shoulder. "Full length mirror's in the back."

I pushed to my feet and went to look, feeling like I was walking into a fog since the smoke seemed to originate from that direction. I had to move at least five pounds worth of dresses that she'd slung over the glass and blink several times to make sense of my reflection.

I mean, it was still summer as far as the weather was concerned, and I spent some time in the sun, but not nearly enough. I didn't exactly qualify as pale, but I never got much darker than freckled anyway. All that, I expected. I was at least two shades paler than I'd been last night, like someone or something had leached the color from my skin. Against that bleached backdrop, my eyes took on a whole new semblance of scary, creepy, Oh. My. God.

By the time I got back to my seat, I had to sit down carefully so as not to miss it and fall on my ass. I kicked Kevin in the shin.

He winced.

"Dude. Why didn't you say something?"

"What did you want me to say? Rude, your freak is getting freakier?"

"Yeah."

"When did you want me to say that? While we were rescuing Amy or while we were at my dad's?"

"I was like this at Amy's?"

"In the car. When Amy and I were fighting."

I should've noticed. Seen my reflection in glass or, for crying out loud, *felt* it. My intuition should've raised an alarm. But it hadn't. Why hadn't it?

"I can handle the eyes," I said. "What is this thing? This new thing?"

The Singer took a deep breath. "I hate to break it to you—"

I interrupted. "Burns talked about mutations when this happened before, in Faery. That's what's happening now, isn't it?"

"Yes," she said.

"What am I changing into?"

"Think a minute."

I didn't want to think. My brain felt kind of foggy. Concentrating took extra effort.

Burns had gone on and on about monsters. About the people with the most power being affected worst. Doing things that couldn't be undone. Horrible things.

No matter how much I couldn't stand some of the fae, I couldn't imagine a Faery King doing terrible things to his people of his own free will. The King would have to have been changed into something the exact opposite of himself. He'd have to have been made into something he hated. Something he feared.

What would a king be afraid of? Nothing. A king had everything. Except...except...

The next thought was just around the corner. I could feel it, but I couldn't see it. I shook my head to clear it. Not that it helped a lot, but I took what I could get.

Focus.

If the same rules applied to me, and Melody's spell was changing me like that, it would have to turn me into my own worst nightmare.

I'd worked harder in the last few years than I ever had in my life to train up right under Oscar. To be a good seer. I'd done it at first because it seemed cool and alternative and I had this gift of magic that scared me. Oscar gave me a framework. Rules.

After the new had worn off, I kept training with him because I wanted to keep the balance between the worlds. I wanted to keep everyone and everything safe.

And now I wasn't safe.

I shuddered and met the Singer's gaze. "Is there any way to stop it?"

She shook her head.

"You're sure?"

She crossed her index finger over her heart. "Sorry."

Kevin looked from me to her and back again. "What'd I miss?"

"The part where I'm turning into some kind of destroyer."

"But you're a protector. That's what you do, man."

"The irony, it burns."

Kev didn't think that was funny. He looked at the Singer. "His eyes and the skin—whatever else—is it something you recognize?"

She nodded. "Demon features. Non-specific, though. Not any particular type of demon I've ever seen."

Oscar said I needed to face my demons before I could become the seer I was meant to be. I never imagined he meant that literally—because he hadn't. This was—I don't know—too on the nose.

Cold sweat slicked the back of my neck. "Fantastic."

"It's not just you."

"Not just me, what?"

Kevin rested his elbows on his knees. "Awesome. Is my consolation prize what I think it is?"

"You get to be one of us, Kev." The Singer tucked a strand of hair behind her ear. "The wings are just the beginning. Pretty soon, you'll start to look at the world a little more objectively."

"What does that mean in human English?" he asked.

"Your emotions will start to matter less. You won't feel as much, except for the most important things. Those, you'll feel so hard you'll be afraid you won't live through the feelings. Then, whatever gift you have inside will surface."

"By gift, you mean something like your voice."

"For you, it will be connected to your ability to hear thoughts. You'll have to use it whether you want to or not. It might not be a good gift, Kevin."

"I might suck at it? Or it might be harmful?"

"Door number two."

Kev stared at the floor while he took it all in. When he glanced up again, his gaze was bleak. "And you? What's going on with you?"

"I'm not sure," she said.

"You have freckles."

"Freckles are not a sign of the apocalypse, Kevin."

"You've never had them before, so maybe they are."

She chewed her bottom lip. "I used to."

"Not since I've known you."

Not since I'd known her, either. Then again, she'd had a life before I met her. A human life.

"No way," I said.

She sighed. "Clearly, there's a way."

Kevin's eyes widened. "You're becoming human again?"

"That's what it seems like," she said. "That's what it feels like. I have no way to confirm. The King would be able to tell me, but I'm cut off until we see this thing through. And we'd better do that fast. Because if I'm fae, I can help you. If I'm human…."

Kevin stood and stepped over the dog, then began to pace. "You could have your life back."

"No." She reached out, laid a hand on his shoulder. "I won't. That life is gone."

"It could be a new one," Kev said. "A good one."

"I don't know how to be human anymore."

"Maybe you don't want to be."

And the conversation had just taken a turn down a street that didn't seem to be about our current situation but totally seemed to be about the Singer and Kevin.

I cleared my throat. "We came here to get you. To bring you back with us to home base at Kev's house. Burns and Reid are picking up the rest of us."

"Then what?"

"We need to go by the scene of the crime and look for clues. Burns and Reid didn't stay long enough to check. Neither did I. We're hoping that there'll be a clue to follow."

"What about the girl who did this?"

"Amy's looking for her."

"Okay," she said. "Why Kevin's house? Home base could be here."

"Here doesn't have enough room for all of us," I said. "Also, there's no bathroom. And my head feels weird. Why do I feel like I'm trying to think through cobwebs ever since we got here?"

"I'm afraid that comes with the territory."

"The destroyer demon territory?"

"All of it, for all of us, actually."

"How am I supposed to figure all this out and turn it around if I can't, well, figure all this out?"

"We," Kev said.

"Fine. We."

"Work fast," she said. "Use what you've got while you've got it."

What did I have? What would be likely to tank first? The stuff that helped me protect people. The stuff that hadn't been a part of me for very long. "My seer skills."

"What about them?"

"I want to try to force a vision. See what I can see." While I still could.

"Now?" Kev asked.

"Is there a better time?"

He stood up. "What do you need?"

"A shot of whisky and a prayer," the Singer said. "You don't have the juice or the control to do it, Rude."

"But I ought to be getting there, right? That's what Oscar said. How it's supposed to work. First the intuition."

"Yours is on the fritz."

I pretended not to hear her. "Can we clear off the rest of this seat? I need room to lie flat."

She and Kev moved the canvases out of the way, stacking them in the back of the bus. They came back with arms full of dresses. Every color and fabric imaginable. Bright yellow wool to black lace.

"Warmest things I've got," the Singer said.

"I don't follow," Kev said.

"His body temperature's gonna drop. That's what happens when you go traveling."

"Traveling?"

"The vision doesn't come to you. You seek it out." She met my gaze. "You do know how to do this?"

I'd never done it before, only approached it in training. "I know how to slow my breathing down. I know what the intuition feels like."

"Good. Tap into however much of it you have left. Follow where it leads you. If you get into trouble, I'll come get you."

"How?"

"I can't follow you exactly, but I can keep tabs on you if I know what you're doing. It's a fae thing, and you're a fae seer, so."

Kevin glanced at her. "Wait. Do I have this fae thing?"

"You will," she said.

"When?"

"When you're close to the point of no return, Kevin."

"Whatever you're gonna do to track him, I want to piggyback."

She nodded. "Ready?"

I lay back on the seat. The Singer and Kevin covered me in layers of wool and lace. Also chiffon and tie-dye and glitter. I closed my eyes and took a deep, patchouli-flavored breath. And another. Every breath deeper. Slower.

I heard the Singer squeeze into the space front of my bench and kneel. The creak of her knees. The rustle of the feathers on her halter. The soft flutter of her wings as they settled against her back. I strained to hear any other sound she made, and instead caught Kevin's shaky inhale. The low noise he made in his throat. The slide of skin on skin. Were they holding hands?

I let go of the question. It was none of my business anyway, and the thought of it reminded me how much the burns on my fingers hurt.

I sank deeper into the weight of my bones on the seat. With each breath in, filling my lungs all the way. With each exhale, going further into the rhythm. In and out. In and out. The thump-thump of my heart. The rush of my blood.

The intuition rose then like a fire inside me, beginning in the pit of my belly and winding up the length of my spine like a snake. It flared in my throat and filled my mouth. When I inhaled again, I breathed it in. When I breathed out, the intuition shot into the space between my eyes and spread out through the crown of my head. The flames furled into the air above me and stretched thin, like gold threads, leading away from me. Three of them. I hadn't expected that.

Follow where it leads you, the Singer had said a few minutes ago. Now, she said it again inside my mind.

How are you here? I asked.

Keeping watch over you, she said.

I could feel Kevin's mind there, too, hovering around her edges.

Which one do I follow? Three threads. I understood—the intuition told me—that I could go with one, not all.

Only you can decide.

Which one? None of them was shinier than the others. No light bulb went off to point the way. What if I chose wrong? What if I missed some vital piece of information?

What if I didn't get any info at all because I couldn't make up my mind?

I went with the one on the left. Thread number one. Followed it up and up through the smoke-tinted air. Through the roof of the bus, into the daylight dappled by the shadows of the warehouses all around. Up and over the asphalt and concrete roofs of the buildings and south beyond the baseball stadium and the elevated freeway. Down towards Westheimer, where the neon lights buzzed to life on the Curve. Antique stores with barren sidewalks. Empty streets.

The thread of intuition led me to the front of the leather bar with the abandoned bikes. And across the street to Snake Bite Tattoo.

Kevin's bike leaned against the outside wall, not chained to anything and ripe for stealing. Except it was outside Malek's, and therefore it belonged to one of his customers, and therefore to steal it would be like taking it from him, and the thief would be in a super-bad way.

There were no thieves anywhere near there, anyhow. Nobody outside. Just Malek and—Amy—inside.

How could Amy be inside? How did she even know about Malek? Because Kevin and I had told her when we filled her in about what happened. She knew who he was. What he was. And she was there anyway.

That could not be good.

I followed the thread inside.

The lobby of Malek's place was empty. Everything in its place. The squeaky clean coffee table. The fanned magazines. The smell of disinfectant, like perfume compared to the sulfur in the outside air. Metallica blared from the speakers. Lights glowed in the back of the shop.

The thread led that direction.

Tracing paper and a spray bottle filled with water sat on the counter with the tattoo equipment. Malek had been drawing. I squinted at the design. Made out a line of rolling waves.

Amy perched on the edge of the vinyl-topped work table. Malek sat on a stool in front of her, writing. I squinted again to make out the words.

I think you were more freaked out than you're letting on. I think you don't have any way to deal with what's happening because you feel too much. You want to help, but you can't, and that makes it worse.

"Because I don't have powers," Amy said.

If you want to stay sane, you'll stay out of this mess. If you want to live, you can stay here until we solve the problem.

She stood up suddenly. "What am I supposed to do? Tell the guy I love to get lost? Watch him and his friends fight to save the world and not lift a finger to help? Pray that everything will be all right? I'm not built that way."

Your friends will have to watch your back when they should be watching their own. One of them is going to get hurt. Or you will, because they won't be able to get to you in time.

She hugged herself.

You know I'm right.

"Hear me out," she said. "I've seen things that aren't supposed to exist. Faeries. Demons. Even you. I've seen last-minute miracles pulled off by luck and smarts and determination so fierce it left me in awe. So maybe you're right. Or maybe I'm that determined, too."

He looked her up and down. Considering. And wrote some more. *What kind of change would you have me make?*

I blinked. Just like that, Amy and Malek had moved. She sat on the workbench again. He'd started his setup. He glanced my direction.

No. Not in my direction—at me. As if he could see me.

A voice bloomed in my mind. *What are you after?*

The sound of it startled me. I'd never heard Malek speak before.

He'd been cursed a long time before I was born—thousands of years, if the stories were true. His voice was gravelly with the weight of all that time, and menacing. Not an immediate threat, but more like a warning not to mess with him, not to double-cross him. As if I would ever be dumb enough to even think about doing something like that.

Then again, I'd told him no. I'd negotiated with him. I owed him.

I'm working on a vision, I said.

You're in my private space.

Vision led me here.

You get what you came for?

I nodded.

Then get outta here. And watch out for Amy. She's gonna need it.

I took a step back. A single step. It was enough to shove me into the lobby of Snake Bite and onto the street. Back toward downtown and into the alley where the Singer's school bus waited. In through the doors and down the smoke-filled aisle. Over the dog and past Kevin and the Singer, who leaned over me and studied my face as if she was looking for something she couldn't find.

My consciousness slammed into my body so hard I felt like I'd been dropped ten stories onto cement. Opening my eyes felt like lifting hundred pound weights. I looked into the Singer's eyes and measured the relief that flooded them.

"I lost you," she said. "Where did you go?"

I opened my mouth, but nothing came out. Words were going to take a while. And I'd been gone a while. From the cast of light inside the bus and what I could see of outside, hours had passed.

I stuttered. "What time is it?"

"Almost 7:00." She took hold of one of my hands.

Kevin grabbed the other. Together, they hauled me upright and then let me go so that I could grab the back of the seat to steady myself. I hung on for dear life.

My breath came fast and shallow. My heart pounded in my chest. The rush of my blood filled my ears. It took everything I had to concentrate on slowing it all down.

Zach stood up from where he'd been lying in the aisle and rubbed against my legs. He whined uneasily. I laid my free hand on his shoulders.

The Singer covered my hand with hers. "Where'd you go, Rude?"

"To the Curve."

"Malek's?" Kevin asked.

"You're not gonna like who I saw there."

He raised a brow.

"Amy. Getting ink."

He stared at me. "Why would she do something like that?"

I didn't want to say. I'd eavesdropped on a private conversation between her and Malek. Her feelings had been super raw. "She wants help. Or she wants to help."

"By getting in deep with a god? What kind of price did he ask her to pay? We have to go get her."

"It's too late," I said. "The deed's done by now."

He swallowed hard. "Is she coming back to the house?"

"She said she was gonna go look for Melody, remember?"

"That's not gonna happen now. She needs to come back home."

The Singer rose, pulling Kevin up with her. "You think you'll, what —pull up beside her and make her get in the car? She's a big girl. Let her do what she can to help."

"She's not like us," Kev said.

"Because she has no magic?" The Singer squeezed his arm. "She's stronger than you think."

"I'm worried," I said.

"You, too?" the Singer asked. "I thought you were smarter than that."

I held up a hand. "Hey, I'm not going there. I'm saying that I went after that vision to get answers to what's happening. To see what I could glean. And the fact that I saw Amy with Malek means something. It's important."

"But you don't know why," the Singer said. "Or what."

"I really don't."

"I hear it in your voice. Confusion."

"Yeah. That's exactly how I feel. It's like that fog from when we were talking before, it's worse or something."

Kevin rubbed the bridge of his nose. "You think the vision caused it?"

I shrugged. "How?"

"No clue. Just that it's the only thing that happened between the first fog and the second. Stands to reason the vision is involved in the fogginess."

"I was using it to help. It's a seer's power."

"The spell Melody did is corrupting your power," he said.

"But I have to use it if we're gonna get through this."

"And if you use it," the Singer said, "you run the risk of getting bad information. Corrupted information, to use Kevin's word."

Not a smiley thought. A worse one came on its heels. I spit it out before I realized what I was saying. "I'm not sure I'd know how to tell the difference."

"You'd know," Kevin said. "Deep down."

I wanted to believe he was right. Wanting didn't make it true. "I'm not so sure."

"Smart enough to know what you don't know. A good place to start." She gave me a small smile in commiseration.

I had a thought that scared me more than all the others. "Potential corruption aside, I have to know—is it gonna be like this every time I use my power? Will the confusion get worse? Does using it make things worse?"

"Maybe," she said. "I wish I could tell you for sure, but there's not a road map, Rude."

"You could try not to use it unless you have to."

I shook my head. "If I have no guarantees, I may as well just do what I can while I can."

She took in my words and the emotions behind them. That was, after all, her magic. "I'll help you. You know that."

"Thanks," I said.

"You know better than that, Rude."

Right. Bad form to thank the fae. Because most humans didn't mean *thank you* as in ongoing gratitude. Most humans meant *thanks, now go away*. Which was rude as hell.

"You know how I meant that."

She laughed. "Just this once."

Kevin flexed his shoulders, which looked super uncomfortable bundled inside cotton and denim. "I hate this."

"Which part?" I asked.

"All of it."

"Why don't you lose the jacket?"

He fidgeted.

"Seriously," I said. "Who's gonna care?"

He peeled off the jacket. Then his T-shirt. He kept his wings furled close to his back, which I appreciated. If he'd stretched them out to full span, the Singer and I would've ended up smacked in the head. Not that she would've noticed. She was staring at his everything.

The Singer reached out to touch his arm. He took a step back.

"I just want to see, Kev. That's all."

He closed his eyes for a moment. When he opened them again, he met her gaze.

She laid her hand on his arm. Ran her fingers along his skin toward his shoulder. Brushed the feathers of the nearest wing with her fingertips.

He blew out a long breath.

"You feel that?" she asked.

He nodded.

"Tell me about it."

"It feels…close."

"Private?" she asked. "Intimate?"

I pushed to my feet. Zach pranced in front of me. "I think we should leave you two alone for a while."

"No," Kevin said. "We should go. All of us. Back to the sidewalk outside the pub, right? If we don't waste any time, we can make it back to the house before dark. Meet up with the crew."

Including Amy.

The Singer pulled her hand away. She tore her gaze away from Kevin and put it on me. Specifically on my hands. "Rude, your fingers."

"What about them?" I looked down.

The burns had healed. No scars. No evidence the burns had ever been there.

I didn't know how to take that. "A good thing, right?"

The Singer didn't answer my question. She said something disturbing instead. "It has to be part of the change."

"The change I don't want. That's happening to me against my will."

"Don't throw the baby out with the bathwater."

"Even if it's a creepy baby?"

Her mouth quirked. "Maybe the burns will come back later."

"You give me hope, Singer."

She sighed. "Let me put on my Docs. Let's find out what we need to do, and get it done."

CHAPTER 6

THE SULFUR STENCH was stronger on the sidewalk outside Rollins Pub. The electrical charge still made all my hair stand on end. The oak that had once been a gate between worlds before it'd been destroyed was gone. Not a single room remained that I could see or feel. It'd been subtracted from the scene. A different thing, one just as magical and unpredictable, had been added.

Melody sat cross-legged with her back against the pub wall, her curves swallowed by baggy overalls. She wore a black tank underneath them, and red hi-top kicks with black laces. She held a lit cigarette in one hand. She didn't appear to have any interest in smoking it, though.

She honed her gaze on me as if her eyes were heat-seeking missiles. She gave Kevin and the Singer and the dog the once-over. Then she stood up, bracing against the bricks. Maybe she thought I'd hurt her. I felt the impulse. The last time I'd seen her, she'd nearly killed me. Her spell disappeared a few million people.

Looking at her felt like looking in a mirror—the kind with razor edges, the kind that would slice you to ribbons with the truth.

I held up my hands to signal a truce.

She took a deep breath and blew it out slowly. "I've been looking for you."

She'd found me easily enough before. "Your faery seer radar broken?"

"You don't show up anymore. It's like you're full of static or something. Like trying to find a radio station but never quite getting it right."

"I've changed."

"Sorry."

"I'm not interested in your apology. What I want is to fix the problem. Is that why you're here?"

She nodded. "You can come closer. I feel fine. No supernova."

I cocked my head to the left. "This is Kevin. Our friend is called the Singer."

"That's a title, not a name. Why wouldn't you want me to know her name?" Melody's eyes widened. "You're fae, right?"

"At the moment," the Singer said.

Melody looked at Kevin. "You're not, though."

"Not yet."

"Don't I know you from school?"

He nodded.

"What happened to you—is it my fault?"

Kevin stretched his wings to full span. Jesus—that had to be six feet across.

"I don't blame you for being mad."

"I'm a lot more than that," he said. "What did you do to us? To the city? What was that spell? Because it was definitely a spell."

She nodded.

I walked over to her. Leaned against the wall beside her. Zach followed me, putting himself between us. She moved her arm to the side, tapping the ashes of her cigarette onto the sidewalk. Zach growled.

Melody eyed the dog and wrapped her arms around herself. "I told you about my dad, the demon. And you know my mom threw me out."

I waited.

"I'm alone," she said. "I don't know how to be alone. I can't take it, Rude."

I couldn't say I understood. I had my own alone issues—my parents didn't see me most of the time. But that was worlds different than what she was going through. I didn't have a stepfather who beat the crap out of me. I didn't have a mom who chose an asshole like that over me. So I didn't say something that would just ring false.

She hugged herself tighter. "I thought, if my mother doesn't want me, maybe he would."

Her demon dad. "So you what—called him?"

"I cast the spell to do it. It's just—that spell? It takes a while to come full circle. Like, seventy-two hours. And it has bad collateral damage."

I blinked at her. "I'm not collateral damage, Melody. I'm a person. Look at me."

She glanced at me sideways. "I know that. I'm sorry. I know that doesn't mean anything, or at least it doesn't mean enough. Not with all of this." She nodded Kevin. At the empty street. The abandoned cars.

"Seventy-two hours," I said. "Three days."

"One of which is already gone." She chewed her lip.

I knew some lore about this kind of thing from my training. There were demons, and then there were Demons. Anything elaborate enough to need that amount of time to summon, with a spell that had side effects like this one, had to be more of a capital D demon.

"Do you know what your father is exactly?"

She shook her head. "I don't think Mom knows either. It wasn't in her diary. She would've written that down, wouldn't she?"

"Did you, like, send a message when you did the casting? Does he know it's you who called?"

"There was no way to tell him," she said. "There were just the steps I was supposed to take."

The Singer came a step closer. She seemed to loom over us. "You found this spell in a book?"

"Yeah. Can you believe it?"

"No, actually."

"Well, I did. Because of Malek. You know him?"

I turned to face her. "He did the ink on your back."

"He told you? Isn't there some kind of tattoo artist-client privilege?"

"He's not a lawyer or a priest," I said. "You get that tattoo as part of the spell?"

She hesitated. "The book said that if I was grounded—if I truly belonged where I called him to—it would boost the magic. Make it stronger."

"You didn't tell Malek about that."

"Wasn't any of his business."

"You're in a world of hurt, lying to him," the Singer said.

"I didn't—"

"Omission is the same as lying."

"What's he going to do? Come after me?"

"Actually," I said, "he sent me after you. He wants you dead."

She slid away from me. "No."

"He wanted me to swear I'd make it happen. I refused."

"No one tells him *no*," the Singer said. "Just like nobody double-crosses that guy and gets away with it."

"I swore something else," I said. "I promised to do justice."

Melody studied my face. She glanced at the Singer. At Kevin. "That's good, right?"

"Depends," Kevin said.

"On what?"

I didn't know, so I didn't answer. Neither did the others.

Melody's mouth trembled, her eyes bleak. "Fine. Okay. So what do we do now?"

"We have to reverse the spell," I said.

"I already told you, Rude. It can't be undone."

"Because the book says so?"

"Yeah."

The Singer closed the distance to Melody. "What's the name of the book?"

Melody flinched from her. "Rude, tell her to get away."

The Singer grabbed Melody by the arms and held on. "You tell us what we need to know."

Melody's voice rose with every word. "*A Compendium of Demonic Magic.*"

The dog growled again. The Singer let go of Melody, who began to shake. The cigarette fell from her fingertips and rolled a few inches, trailing a ribbon of toxic smoke.

Poison, that was what it was. I had a sudden urge to quit. To never smoke again. It was a good urge, but I needed to focus.

I remembered seeing the book Melody named in Oscar's bookcase. I remembered touching it. It was smaller than most of the others. Bound with leather. Pages old and wrinkled.

I met Melody's gaze. "You stole the book."

"You're telling me what I did. You're not even asking?"

"Don't lie to me, too."

She nodded. "I got it from the other seer's house. Your boss."

"Was he home when you took it?" I asked.

"If he was, he didn't come in the room or say anything. The house felt empty to me."

"Because he's gone," I said. "He didn't tell anybody where he was going or when or why. If you did something to him—"

She interrupted. "What could I do to somebody like that? He's too powerful."

The Singer shook her head. "In case you didn't notice, so are you."

"I'm not that smart. He is."

"How'd you get in?" I asked.

"Through the back window."

I hadn't seen one open, but maybe she'd closed it behind her when she left. "Where's the book now?"

"At Beth's house, where I've been staying."

"Beth Barrett?"

"Take us there," the Singer said.

Melody raised her hands, covering her eyes. "I can't go back there. I can't go anywhere. I want to run."

"Try it and I won't hesitate to take you to Malek."

Melody looked from the Singer to me. "Would you let her do that, Rude?"

I wouldn't wish that fate on my worst enemy. I didn't want Melody to think that was what we were—enemies. But she had to understand we meant business. "I wouldn't stop her."

"That's hard."

A nerve-shredding caw sounded overhead. From the throat of a single crow perched on the pub's roof. It looked me in the eye. Interested. Yeah, definitely interested.

I glanced at Kevin. Pointed at the bird.

Before Kev could open his mouth, it flew away, the flap of its wings in the air louder than they should've been.

I felt something tug at me—Melody's gaze.

I looked at her. "That's the way it is. Are you going with us to Beth's house or not?"

"Do I have a choice?"

"There's always a choice."

A single tear rolled down her cheek. "She's home, just so you know. At least, she was when I left."

"She normal?" Kevin asked.

"So far."

I pointed to the Explorer. "Let's go."

We sat her in the back between the Singer and Kevin. Less chance she'd try to bolt that way. Zach rode shotgun. The sun set as we drove, the sky turning pink and orange and gold before the darkness took over completely—a reminder that some beauty remained in the world. I held on to it as if it were a sign. As if it were hope itself.

Beth lived in one of the new houses behind the high school. Swankier neighborhood than mine, where the houses were big enough—these came with stuff like servant's quarters. I couldn't wrap my mind around needing that. Around wanting that.

Beth's place was blue with white trim, and two stories with one of those balconies upstairs that some people called a veranda, complete with flowery outdoor furniture and wide-blade ceiling fans that spun in lazy circles as we drove up and parked. Year-old oaks had been planted in the yard. Yellow blooms dotted a flowerbed that ran the length of the house.

Melody had a key, but she knocked anyway.

Beth answered the door in a *Star Trek II: The Wrath of Khan* T-shirt and a pair of holey jeans. Scuffed, white sneakers with no socks. Her brown hair hung in six thick braids down to her shoulders. Her silver-framed glasses had slid halfway down her nose. She pushed them back into place with her index finger.

She narrowed her eyes at Melody. "No more explodey shenanigans?"

"Not today."

"But you brought company?"

"From school. Well, two out of three."

Beth did a double-take at me. "Rude? Is that you? And Kevin? And who's that?"

Meaning the Singer. "A friend."

"Wow. Nice halter. I'm a fan of peacocks. Except when they sing. Have you ever heard one of them sing? Fingernails on a chalkboard. Oh, and hey, nice dog."

Zach wagged his tail.

I started to say something about the way we looked. To explain.

She waved me off. "No worries. As long as you're not fixin' to put any hurt on me, you can come in."

"You're not afraid of us?" Kev asked.

"Have you seen what's going on out there? I've checked out, like, a ten-block radius, and there's almost no one left. The ones that are still around? Hey, they've got similar problems to you guys, but they're too freaked to do anything except run away from me. I got no idea how things got this way, but I'm betting a million you're here to tell me. Right? So, yeah, re: afraid. But we got bigger problems." She turned on her heel with a squeak of rubber sole on waxed hardwood and walked away.

Melody followed, and we followed Melody into the foyer, which had a spiral staircase and a thirty-foot ceiling. An enormous fireplace took up the far corner—maybe they used it in February, when it actually got cold around here. A thick Oriental rug and two small leather sofas took up the space in front of it. A low, cherry coffee table crouched between them.

Melody sat on the edge of the table. She was the only one who actually did. The rest of us loitered. Except the dog, who hung on Beth's heels as she disappeared behind what looked like a glassed-in wine room and into the kitchen.

"Y'all want something to drink?" she called.

The sooner we got out of there, the sooner we could get home to Amy. Or find her. I wanted the book, and then I wanted gone. I could see from Kev's expression that he felt the same. The Singer had other ideas.

"Whisky," she said.

Beth's giggle was full of nerves. "Irish?"

"Fine."

Beth emerged from the kitchen with a tray stacked with five short tumblers and a bottle of Jameson. She set the tray down on the table and poured each of us two fingers.

The Singer downed hers in one swallow, then set her glass down on the table. "Hit me again."

Beth raised an eyebrow, but she poured another shot.

This time, the Singer sipped. "You know why we're here?"

"Miserable as Melody looks, I'm guessing it's because you know she's the source of all things screwed up. And you want our help."

"Hers, actually," I said. "No offense."

"Who do you think found the book for her? Who do you think picked the lock on that house? Wasn't her. She's, like, helpless."

I stared at her. "You did those things?"

"Stop looking at me like I'm some kind of alien. I was bored. It seemed like fun."

Kevin stretched his wings wide. "Bored?"

"Seriously?" Beth sighed. "I'm taking six classes this semester and

I'm acing all of them. Plus the extracurricular stuff—Chess Club, Chemistry Club, volunteering at the food bank. Mom's trying to keep me busy. And she's trying to make sure that I get into the 'university of my choice.' That's exactly how she says it. Can you believe? Anyway, I'm bored to fucking tears. And Melody came to live with us, which was cool and all. She asked me to solve a mystery with her— you know, about her dad—how could I say no? And if there was hacking involved, or a little B&E, bonus."

Now Kevin was the one staring. "What are you? Some kind of criminal mastermind?"

"I'm seventeen," Beth said.

"Non-sequitur."

"It's the only sequitur I've got."

"You didn't think about the consequences?" he asked.

"I was thinking about the fun."

"Demons aren't fun."

Beth took a sip of her whisky and coughed. "Ugh. Embarrassing. Not much of a drinker, I admit. Though I'm practicing."

"That's between you and your liver," the Singer said. "Since we know you're part of this bullshit, you're in for helping us fix it, whether you like it or not."

"Threats? I hate threats."

The Singer smiled. Not in a friendly way. "Then think of it as a promise."

Beth took another drink. This time, she managed not to cough, although her face turned two shades of pink. "Okay. Now what?"

"We need to see the book," I said. "Can you get it for us?"

"Sure. It's in my room. BRB."

In case she had no intention of being right back, I walked after her up the winding staircase and past the family room with a big screen TV large enough to take up most of the wall and into a maze of bedrooms. The lights blazed bright in every one of them. I guessed her mom didn't worry about the electric bill. Or Beth was afraid of the dark.

She threw a glance over her shoulder. "Conspicuous consumption, I know."

"What?"

"My mom has more money than sense. It's just the two of us. We don't need all this space. But it makes her feel better."

"Not judging."

"Of course you are. Everybody does."

"You live here. It's your home."

"It's my fourth home in twelve years. And I'm an environmentalist."

Of course she was. That was why she'd hooked up with Melody to summon a demon. Environmentalists did that sort of thing all the time.

Her room was the third one on the right. *Trek* posters lined three walls. A bookcase took up the fourth. A blue rag rug warmed up the floor. A denim comforter and a mass of matching decorative pillows covered the full-sized bed.

She peeled back the comforter, dumping half the pillows on the floor. She lifted the mattress and reached under it, pulling out the book. It looked exactly the way I remembered. She held it out.

I took it. It felt heavy. And kind of alive, as if it had a mind of its own—and it was checking me out. Paying attention to the temperature of my hand. Whether my palm sweated. How tightly I held it. What my intentions were.

"You notice anything funny about this book?" I asked.

"Besides the part where it's full of magic spells?"

I nodded.

"It smells strange."

I raised the volume to my face. Breathed in. "Smells like an old book."

"In your experience, do old books try to put you to sleep while you're trying to read them?"

"Most books do that to me."

"Right. You're the party guy. Class clown. Probably you never read."

"I read to find out stuff. Then I'm done. I don't have to like it."

"Your loss," she said. "Anyway, that book? The times I've read it, it's like I can't keep my eyes open for more than two paragraphs. Like it's trying to keep me from figuring out what's inside. Maybe it's got some spell on it as well as in it. You know, something designed to keep people from reading it?"

I'd never heard of a spell like that, but then again, I was still learning. And if the book had spells in it that could summon demons, and if Oscar kept that book safe in his library, then maybe Oscar had spelled it to keep people's prying eyes the hell out.

"When did you notice that?" I asked.

"First time I picked it up. At that house."

"Should've been your first clue."

"I'm not stupid, you know."

"Of course not," I said. "You're super smart in all the ways that the university of your choice will love. But in my world, you're not exactly on top of the mountain."

"What world is that?"

"The one with the demons and faeries. I deal with magic every day. It's real. You need a different kind of smart."

"Street smart?"

"I see you've heard of it."

"You don't have to be an asshole, Rude."

Actually, it felt like I did. But I didn't want to be—it was against my nature. The two emotions warred in my chest, and I hated the way it felt. Not to mention the big bite of fear that I suddenly seemed to have become stuck in my throat. Two words filled my mind.

Demon. Destroyer.

I spoke from between clenched teeth. "Sorry."

"You're scary. You know that?"

"I feel scary. Let's go downstairs and you can show us the exact spell you two used. Yeah?"

"Fine, but you go first."

"Why?"

"Because I don't want you walking behind me. It's too creeptastic."

The hairs on the back of my neck stood straight up. I looked over my shoulder at her twice to make sure she followed. She made nervous, silly faces at me both times. It didn't help. In fact, it made me feel worse.

The book in my hand felt like it was trying to tell me something. Like it had a voice that whispered in my ear. I didn't understand the language.

If I could get the gist, would it be good or bad? A book like this, there could only be one answer.

I wanted only to put it down. I picked up the pace until I reached the bottom of the stairs, then shooed Melody off the coffee table so I could drop the book. The second the leather left off contact with my skin, the whispering stopped. The feeling of being seen and judged vanished.

"Show me," I said.

Beth hunkered down and flipped through the pages. "There. Page seventy-eight."

I peered at the text. The spell took up two pages. Hard to read. Made me want to take a nap. *Huh.*

The spell included a long list of instructions. Things that had to be done in order before the magic could even be called up.

Do magic to become part of the land. Melody had gone to Malek for ink.

Spill your blood on the spiritual center of that land to compel its help.

I looked at Melody. "What's this?"

She grimaced. "You know where the spiritual center of the land is, right? I mean, your boss would've showed you."

I had to think about it, and think hard. Oscar had taken me downtown once near the beginning of my training. There was a willow in Tranquility Park on top of a hill near the fountain pool. Oscar said that the tree was important.

Trees were priests. They moved the energy of the underworld through our world. Their branches reached toward heaven. And some trees, like the oak near the pub—ground zero—served as portals.

The willow served as the heart of the city.

"The willow, but it's not there anymore," I said. "Hurricane Ike took it down."

She nodded. "In the physical world."

"What's that mean?" Kevin asked.

"That the willow still exists," I said. "Just not as bark and leaves. It's a ghost."

He pushed the hair back from his forehead. "Trees have ghosts. Really?"

"In this case, yeah," Melody said. "If you look sideways, you can see it."

Beth reached behind to scratch her own back. "What's *look sideways?*"

The Singer answered. "A lot of people think that to see into other worlds, you have to do all this elaborate shit. That's not necessarily so. To get there bodily, sure. That's big work. But seeing inside isn't so complicated. You've heard that there are veils between the worlds, right? Barriers?"

Beth shook her head. "I never heard any of this stuff until Melody started sleeping on the sofa."

The Singer stared at her. "You're taking all of this way too easy. Not nearly enough freak-out. Not any, actually."

"Maybe I'm in shock."

"Or you're lying," the Singer said.

Beth crossed her arms over her chest. "Fuck you."

"Would that be *fuck you for insulting me* or *fuck you for seeing through my bullshit and calling me on it?*"

Beth looked away. Only for a second, but that was long enough for me know we were looking at door number two.

"Spill," I said.

"I had a traumatic childhood."

"What kind of trauma?" I asked.

"I was bored, like I said." She let her hands fall to her sides. "So I investigated a lot of things. Like the number of microbes in the soil and all the different types of birds in the backyard and how to cook and bake stuff because it's not like Mom was ever home to do it. Also, the occult."

"Dude. I love how you tacked that on at the end. Like the occult is the same as learning how to bake cookies."

She grinned at me. It came out more like a grimace. "It was all books. Coded instructions on how to do magic with esoteric ingredients. Overblown stories. I thought they were exaggerating."

"So," the Singer said, "when Melody came, it stopped being pretend —or theoretical—and started being real."

Beth walked around us and plopped down on the empty arm of the sofa. "I thought it was awesome. Except for the part where real means, you know, real. The spell was fun and all, but after? I never expected all this."

I did my best to look reassuring. Not so easy with demon eyes and the super pale skin. But I tried. "We need to go to the tree."

Beth furrowed her brow.

"It'll be all right," I said.

She reached for the coffee table. Knocked wood.

CHAPTER 7

T HE PUDDLED LIGHT OF STREETLAMPS marked the edges
of the park. The rest of it lay in shadow.

Old oaks stood sentry, guarding the darkness, the sidewalk no match for the strength and will of their roots. Hundreds of crows stained their branches black. The noise of the damned birds drowned out all other sound, even the rhythmic song of toads and cicadas. Towering behind the trees, the tall silver fountains that had been shut down for the night looked like giant bullets, the pools of water at their feet oily and murky.

The park knew we'd gathered there to do something big. Like the book, it was a sentient being. It held its breath, waiting for us to make a move.

Kevin stood to my left, Melody to my right. Beth and the Singer hung back a bit with the dog, who'd barked and charged the windows when we'd tried to leave him in the car. In my magical mind's eye, each of them had their own color, their own scent.

Kev was white, the same color as his wings. He smelled like a pile of leaves on a blustery fall day. Melody? Red and sulfur-tainted. Beth smelled like a library and the air around her glowed a yellow like the midday sun. If you stayed in its heat and light too long, it burned.

The Singer was a spinning column of blinding blue light that reminded me of melting ice. She smelled like a winter day at the beach —all salt air and chilled north wind.

The dog looked and smelled just like himself. Nothing concealed behind his shaggy-dog exterior.

It had to mean something that I could see and smell all of that. Magic, growing stronger within me. But was it seer's power, or a demon's?

Whatever it was, I would have to use it and deal with the consequences later. My friends needed me. The city and everyone in it needed me. I wouldn't let them down.

I scanned the park until I saw the shadow of the hill where the willow had stood once upon a time. The back of my neck itched. The hairs on my arms stood up like antennae.

"Anyone else feel that?" I whispered.

Kevin's wing nudged my shoulder. "Like we've got a target on our backs?"

Exactly. "Melody, did you do anything here you didn't tell us about?"

"Only what the spell called for. You read it."

Pouring her blood at the foot of the tree. Making herself part of the land. Making it possible for her to summon her demon dad.

I took a step toward the hill. The ground shook under me. A small tremor.

"Y'all feel that?" I asked.

"Check," Kevin said.

A second step. Another tremor. Stronger this time. The whole park reverberated with a low moan.

The Singer's voice rose behind me. "Something's wrong, Rude. This shouldn't be happening."

I glanced at Melody. She didn't return the favor. In fact, she seemed to be trying real hard not to look at me. She lit a cigarette instead.

Whatever she'd done, it'd been more than just making herself part of the land. She'd altered something fundamental in the land itself.

Could the city have been Gothamed if she hadn't changed the foundation beneath it? And why had it taken so long for me to realize that?

"Melody?"

She studied her shoes.

The tremors underfoot grew stronger, and I understood it for the warning it was. Either we ignored it and raced ahead, or we turned back and tried again later—but there might not be a later. We only had so much time.

There were a lot of steps between here and the hill. A lot of chances for whatever waited for us to put us in a world of hurt. If something happened to me, I could deal. If something happened to my friends?

I took off at a full run.

Kevin yelled behind me. My name. Assorted curse words.

I didn't look back. I poured on the speed instead, sneakers slapping the concrete. The earth shook again—and, this time, it didn't stop.

My ankle twisted. I went down like a sack of rocks. Pushed to my feet again. Ignored the shooting pain and kept running down the sidewalk. I launched myself onto the incline and belly-flopped onto the grass, clawing for a handhold. I half-crawled and half-climbed to the top.

The place where the willow had once been sat empty. Grass filled in where the City had pulled the stump. Somebody had slept there recently. They'd left a blanket roll and an empty plastic water bottle that rattled as the earth quaked.

My ankle screamed. My heart pounded. The rush of blood in my ears drowned out everything except the park's moans. Something— someone—shoved into me from behind, knocking me on my face. They grabbed me by the shoulder and pulled me up again.

Melody, her face a mask of pain. Whatever the park did to me, it'd clearly done something much worse to her. Was still doing it.

She spoke in my ear. "Look sideways."

I closed my eyes.

A winding fire of intuition flowered in the pit of my belly. Shot up the length of my spine until it burned behind my eyes. I opened them again. Looked from the corner of my eye.

The willow's thick trunk swayed in the wind. Its long tendril branches whipped at my face. The earth around its roots looked stone cold dead. Not a single blade of grass. Not one insect.

I heard the tree's voice inside my head, menace in its words. *I remember you. You came once with the seer. You never came again.*

I'm here now.

Too late.

I know what happened here. At least, I know part of it. The girl next to me did something bad. Something evil.

Then why have you brought her with you?

To help put things right again.

It cannot be done.

That's what she says. I've been in awful situations before, though, and I've always found a way to solve the problem. There's got to be a way here.

The only way out is through.

What does that mean?

You must complete the spell.

Summon the demon?

Only then can the demon be defeated and order be restored.

No. This needed to end before the demon got here. That kind of power—how could I possibly fight of that? Hell, how could *we* do it? We had a lot of talent, but this was way beyond our collective skill.

There's no other way?

No.

It'll put everything back the way it was?

No. That can never be done.

The words made my heart hurt.

This is your responsibility, seer. It is your magic to wield and to right.

The tree quieted. It wouldn't speak again. I knew it in my bones, in my heart, in my blood.

I let my intuition guide me back to the hill, to the grass I knelt on, to the wind that lifted the tail of my shirt and cooled my sweat.

The earth had stopped shaking. The night filled with the rustle of leaves and branches in the breeze, the pop of crow wings catching air as they took flight. Frog and cicada song reasserted itself, swelling to fill my head.

Melody spoke, her voice husky and empty. "Where did you go?"

"What do you mean?"

"You disappeared. How did you do that? You were just supposed to look sideways."

"I talked to the willow."

"You're different again. Your hair."

I reached for the top of my head. "What about it?"

"It's white, Rude."

Footfalls sounded behind us. Three sets of feet, human and dog, on the bridge. I smelled them at the same time I heard them.

"This is bad," Melody said. "Real bad."

"I agree." The Singer stepped onto the incline behind us and climbed up. I sensed her blinding blue light without having to look, just like before. I focused on it until her combat boots came even with me. "Can you stand up, Rude?"

I tried, starting with my good ankle. While I pushed to my feet, Kevin came up behind me. He gave me a winged shoulder to lean on.

"Tell us what happened," he said.

"Not until Melody here tells us why she lied. She did a lot more than pour out her blood."

She shook her head. "No."

"It's your word against the willow's. I can't think of a reason for the tree to lie. Can you?"

Her shoulders dropped. "No."

I raised a brow. Was it white, too? Or was only the hair on top of my head bleached by magic?

Melody glowed a darker red in my sight. "I couldn't take the risk that what I did would be reversed. I needed the spell to work. I needed my father to be able to come. I knew you would try to stop it, Rude. That's how you are."

"That's my job," I said.

"It's more than that. You're like some kind of Hawaiian-shirt-wearing hero. You don't stop until you make it right."

"How would you know that? You don't really know me."

"How long have we gone to school together?" she asked.

I shrugged. "High school."

"Longer than that. You just don't remember me."

"I remember everybody."

"Since you started training to be a seer, but not before."

I thought back. Maybe my elephant memory wasn't a lifelong gift. Maybe it, like my luck, had something to do with the training, like she said.

"You might not have known who I was, but I knew who you were. God, I even had a crush on you."

How was a dude supposed to take that? My face flushed hot. A million dollars, my ears and neck had turned bright pink.

"You were larger than life," she said.

"That's because I'm tall."

"It's because you're you."

She hadn't come along because we'd threatened her or because she wanted to help. She'd come because she needed to make sure her work—the damage she'd done—remained intact.

Kev and the Singer hemmed her in, closing any space she could run through.

I took a step toward her. Got in her face. "How did you change the land?"

"The tattoo—it was a link to the city, to the land. It was a kind of doorway that Malek made for the city to find me and claim me so that I belonged to it. So I'd have a home."

Right. "All of which we already know."

"That kind of doorway is like those portals you guard, Rude. Like the oak tree in front of the pub?"

"A portal like that goes both ways." From the city to Melody, and from Melody to the city. The city had given her a home. What had she given to the city?

She undid the hooks on the bib of her overalls and tied them around her waist. She reached over her shoulders and pulled up the back of her tank. It looked like one of Malek's tattoos—full of life and movement—until her shirt rose above the center of her back. A thick, shiny, red welt rose from the skin there. Obliterated the pattern of the ink.

I took a step toward her. My legs shook, but they held. I reached to touch the welt. She drew a sharp breath.

The heat of her skin took me by surprise. Warm as they were, my fingers might as well have been ice against her. She sank into my touch as if she didn't mind it. More, as if she wanted it. That surprised me. And it triggered an avalanche of feelings out of nowhere. Completely inappropriate feelings.

I put them out of my mind and forced my attention where I needed it to be.

The welt had to be a half-inch higher than the skin around it. I thought at first that the shine had to be from oil or ointment or something she'd put on it to help it heal, but it didn't feel greasy. It felt raw.

My voice shook. "A brand?"

"It burned like a motherfucker."

"You did it yourself? Or did somebody help you?"

Beth chimed in fast. "Wasn't me."

I glanced at her. Her eyes were wide behind her glasses and her mouth had fallen open. She looked sunshine yellow around the edges. Clear and bright. Telling the truth.

"I did it myself," Melody said. "The spell said I had to."

"You find it in the same book?"

"Yeah." She dropped her shirt. Untied the tabs of her overalls and put herself together again.

"What'd you use?"

She turned to face me slowly. "Tire iron."

Kevin gasped behind me.

"It was the only thing I had that was big enough, and I needed it to be made of metal so I could get it hot enough."

The whole idea of her taking a tire iron to her own flesh made my whole body crawl. "Not with a normal fire, you didn't. Magic needs more than that."

She touched the tip of her index finger to her nose. "Can't get anything past you, can I? A normal fire would get it hot enough, but not in the right way. It had to be a special fire. It had to have a little of the same magic Malek used in his ink. There's a spot in the upper left corner, where the tattoo wraps over my shoulder. I stuck a needle in it when I got home from Snake Bite, to open it up while the ink was still fresh. I used tweezers to take a pinch of ink and skin. I saved it to add to the fire when the time was right."

She'd made the city demonic. That was what she'd given it in return for its gift to her.

Melody thinned her lips. "I had to make sure you couldn't reverse my magic, and from the look on your face, you can't. Can you?"

I shook my head.

The Singer's voice held the energy of a command. "We take her to Malek now."

Melody's skin began to radiate heat. "No."

"No," I echoed.

The Singer narrowed her eyes. "What?"

"We need her. We have to complete the spell. That's what the willow told me. We have to let the demon come and then defeat it. Melody comes with us."

"You can't make me," she said.

The Singer's words wrapped Melody in magic that no amount of heat could break. The words entered Melody's ears, holding her, binding her. "Shut up and do what I tell you."

We headed back to the Explorer slowly and carefully. My ankle wouldn't allow much more than that. When we'd parked it across the street, we'd been alone. There hadn't been a single soul nearby, but there was somebody there now.

Malek leaned against the passenger door, arms at his sides, hands curled into fists. He bristled with pent-up rage. It flowed off his muscled arms, off the gleaming top of his head. He smelled like blood.

He pushed away from the car and I saw it. A single slice across the belly. The stain of red on his white shirt. The smears on his black leather pants. Spots on his boots.

I couldn't see the wound through the hole in his shirt.

He saw the question on my face and unclenched his fists so that he could sign an answer. *I heal fast.*

"That happen tonight?"

An hour ago.

"Was it deep?"

Mortal, he signed. *If I were mortal.*

The Singer wove her way up to the front of the pack and stood beside me. "Serpent," she said.

He inclined his head. *Peacock. I see you've brought me a prize.*

It struck me that the Singer possessed the very thing that had been taken from him. The voice that persuaded. The voice that seduced. The ability to make people feel whatever she wanted them to, which in her case usually amounted to their fiercest desire. I wondered if he hated her.

Somebody sent an assassin to take me out. Who would be that stupid?

Nobody with a brain. Or even a brain stem.

I caught a glimpse of horror on Melody's face before she locked it down behind the mask of innocence I'd already seen way too much. "You?"

She didn't answer.

"I just asked you up there if there was anything else I needed to know. You said no."

She looked at her feet. Paced a quick circle. Glanced at me. "I meant it."

"Clearly, you left out this one small point."

"You said he wanted me dead. You said nobody double-crosses him and lives to tell about it. I don't want to die."

"Clearly, you do," I said.

"I built a magical being. A construct. I gave it one job. Clearly, it didn't have enough juice."

Malek signed. Kevin translated. "Way dead. Cut into small pieces and scattered out back for the crows. They've probably eaten what's left of him by now."

"Kevin, you couldn't understand sign language to save your life back at Snake Bite. All of a sudden, you're an expert?"

"I don't know. I mean, I'm not reading the signs. I'm reading what's behind them."

Behind them. "Thoughts? Emotions?"

"They're popping into my head. Like pictures in my mind."

"Dude."

"I know."

"That's fae."

"I. Know."

I didn't want to wrap my head around that. I couldn't get stuck on it either. Too much I didn't get. Too much at stake.

"You think you deserve mercy?" I asked.

She didn't hesitate. "No. I'll take justice. Isn't that what you promised?"

I turned to face Malek. "I did. I gave you my word."

I remember, he signed.

"You still believe I'm good for it?"

If I didn't, we wouldn't be having this conversation at all.

No, we wouldn't. I'd be in the same place as the assassin. Food for blackbirds.

I could be an apprentice for only so long before I had to take the reins as a seer. Power and responsibility. My word was my bond in every realm. I knew it. Malek knew it. So why had he come here?

"Did you think I'd hand her over to you?"

It was worth a shot.

Nice joke. Probably nobody else saw it that way. Maybe the Singer understood. A glance out of the corner of my eye brought her smile into focus. She seemed to have too many teeth one second, and looked human the next.

"What do you want, Malek?" I asked.

I want in.

'In' meant what? Hanging out? Figuring out? Running into disaster with us? "Keeping an eye on me? Making sure I follow through?"

Making sure she does.

"Okay." I didn't give the others a say. It wouldn't matter what they thought, only what Malek did. They couldn't stop him. None of them would try. "You riding with us, or did you bring your own transportation?"

He hooked a thumb over his shoulder at a shape I could just make out—a motorcycle parked twenty feet in front of the Explorer. The bike pinged my magical sight. It had a halo of its own, one that looked like bloody mist. For a moment, I considered asking about that, but we had too many fish to fry and of course Malek would drive a magical machine, right?

I nodded. "Excellent. "We're going back to Kevin's. It's our home base. The others should be there by now. You need directions?"

I'll follow you.

"Wait," Kevin said. "I want to ask about Amy."

Annoyance flashed across Malek's face. *I helped her.*

"By working magic on her? Don't you think we've got enough of that going around? You changed her."

She asked me to.

"Don't you need a better reason than that?"

Not in her case.

Kevin advanced on Malek. Didn't stop until they were nose to nose. "What's that supposed to mean?"

Fear spiked the pit of my belly. At what Kev would do. At what Malek might do to him.

The god didn't take the bait. *She needed my help. She's a part of this even though she shouldn't be. I couldn't refuse her. That's all you need to know.*

Kevin drew back his hand. Slammed his palm against the car window so hard he rattled the glass. He stood rooted to the spot, bristling. Malek didn't move a muscle. He didn't even twitch.

"I need a lot more than that," Kev said.

I'll rephrase. That's all you get to know.

And that, beloved people, was as far as I was willing to let this run. "We should go."

Still, neither of them moved.

I scrubbed the top of my head. "Kev?"

He turned to look at me. "Yeah. Okay."

I allowed myself to feel relieved for, like, ten seconds. All the time I was willing to take. "Everybody in the car."

I slid into the driver's seat and turned the headlights on as soon as the engine gunned to life, just in time to see Malek slip on a helmet. Kind of funny, really. I mean, it was the law, but who'd be enforcing tonight? He didn't need the protection. If he had to lay down the bike, he'd walk away with a scratch that would heal faster than we could get him bandaged up.

"This is so not awesome," Beth said from the back seat.

I gazed into the rearview mirror. Beth had gathered her knees to her chest. The dog pressed up against her, smudging her glasses with his wet nose.

"Who is that guy?" she asked.

"A god," Kevin and the Singer said simultaneously.

The god pulled away from the curb and I followed suit, hitting the gas to put us in front of him.

Kevin grabbed the back of my seat. "You realize what this means, don't you?"

A thousand, million different shitty things. "We're bringing Malek to your house. Your dad is gonna freak out."

Who else would be at Kevin's house by the time we got there? The fae cops. Scott and Stacy. Possibly the Singer's father. And Kevin's girlfriend, who'd told us she was going to find Melody but rode her bike straight to Snake Bite for magic ink and heaven only knew what else.

I felt pretty sure about the *what else*. Malek could've opened up about his conversation with her, even with Kevin in his face. He could've calmed the sitch with a handful of words, but he'd chosen the opposite.

My visionary skill set still left a lot to be desired. I didn't know how many things I'd missed when I followed that thread and saw Amy with Malek. But I knew them both.

Neither of them backed down, ever. Neither of them took no for an answer.

And that scared the hell out of me.

CHAPTER 8

W E FOUND AMY sitting cross-legged on Kevin's porch, clothes rumpled and hair wild, smelling like she'd taken a bath in chlorine. The overhead light buzzed and flickered. Moths circled, battered their winged bodies against the glass to find a way in, proof that instinct could kill.

She looked wrong, but she was here. "It's good to see your face."

"Yours is scary."

"So I've heard. How long have you been waiting out here?"

She furrowed her brow. "An hour? Maybe two."

"You didn't ring the bell?"

"It's the middle of the night, Rude. I don't have a key and I didn't want to wake anybody. Besides, I didn't see your car yet. I figured you'd be back soon." She studied her nails. Eight out of ten had been bitten to the quick. She went to work on number nine.

I'd never seen her do that before. Even in the thick of trouble, I'd never seen her that nervous.

Kevin stepped around me and knelt beside her, folding his wings tight against his back. "Are you all right?"

She peeled off the end of her fingernail with her teeth. "Why wouldn't I be?"

He took her face in his hands. "I need you to tell me what happened."

"I guess it won't do any harm now, but can we have the conversation indoors?"

She let him help her up and stood behind him while he unlocked the door. She kept her shoulders squared, refusing to look any direction other than forward. Refusing to look back at the Singer.

The squeal of the hinges sounded extra-loud in the silence of the entry. So did the squeak of the floorboards under our feet. A towering shape popped up from the sofa in the living room. A hand reached from it to the table lamp. Flicked on the light.

Scott. He was an inch shorter than my six-three, less Hawaiian-shirt-wearing party dude and more black-and-white-rugby-shirt-wearing jock. His jeans had permanent grass marks at the knees from the pickup football games he played. His sneakers were scuffed from contact with the concrete basketball court behind the school. A shock of his blond hair stuck up at a weird angle in the back.

I pointed that out with a passing glance. He smoothed it out with a big hand.

"I had second watch," he said.

"Good job falling asleep."

"I'm living my best life. Hey, Kev—your dad went to sleep. Actually, I carried him to his bed and put him in it after he fell asleep. He wanted to see you get home. Lame, I know."

"Thanks, man."

"No worries."

Kevin took off down the hall toward his dad's room.

"What time is it?" Scott reached for a puddle of silver links on the table beneath the lamp. His watch. "3:30. Nice."

"We got sidetracked," I said.

"Always. Listen, those cops are sacked out at the breakfast table and Stacy's in Kevin's room. They couldn't find Mr. Nance. I should say *we* couldn't find him. We tried." He met the Singer's gaze. "Sorry."

"That's all right," she said, although it couldn't be.

If they hadn't been able to find Nance, it would be because he was one of the missing.

Scott slipped his watch onto his wrist. "I'm going to go make some coffee. You assemble the team?"

I made my way to Kev's room. Before I could open the door all the way, Stacy sat up in the bed, her blond curls a rioting halo. She'd slept in her clothes. Her long purple skirt tangled up with her legs, her black tee rumpled.

"We need a better plan next time," she said. "Too much time twiddling our thumbs until you got back. Okay?"

"Okay." I found her Birkenstocks on the rug near the foot of the bed. I handed them to her so she could slip them on.

She followed me into the kitchen, yawning with sound effects. We were the last to arrive. The darkness outside, the early morning stillness—the only sounds were quiet conversation and the burbling of the coffee maker.

The cops had been roused at the table. Impressions from the placemats marked their cheeks.

"That's a good look for you two," I said.

Officer Burns scowled. "Piss off."

Scott had made sure everybody who wanted a cup had one in hand. Mr. Landon sipped from a cracked, economy-sized mug. A piece of tissue stuck to the stubble on his face. Beside him, Kevin leaned against the wall with Amy in his arms. She fidgeted as my gaze passed over her. Not because of me—not that I could tell, anyway. Kevin seemed to be holding onto her more tightly than she'd like.

The Singer sat on the counter next to Malek with the book in her lap. Melody and Beth sat on the floor at their feet. Beth took off her glasses, huffed moisture on the lenses, and wiped them with the hem of her shirt. Melody picked at a weak spot in the tile floor, on her way to making a decent-sized hole.

Stacy and I took up position on either side of Scott near the coffee maker. I drank the muddy dregs of the pot and brought everyone up to speed with help from Kev and the Singer.

I choked on the last sip. Pounded my chest with my fist. "So that's where we're at."

Mr. Landon shook his head. "This is crazy."

Kevin closed his eyes. "Dad—"

"I'm just saying."

"You still holding down the fort?"

Mr. Landon buried his face in his mug.

I cleared my throat. "Melody, you said before that the spell had to be completed within seventy-two hours."

She sighed. "There are three more steps. And thirty-six hours."

The Singer flipped open the book to the spell. Every muscle in her body seemed to relax, legs wobbling as if they might give way. She blinked hard, snapping herself back to attention. "Wow."

"Sleepy, right?" Beth asked. "I wasn't kidding."

The Singer popped Beth in the back of the shoulder with the tip of her boot.

Beth swatted at her.

The Singer bent closer to the book. "Invoke the demon. That's next."

"Does it say how?" I asked.

"In detail. We'll need some supplies. They'll have to be gathered from all over town."

I wanted the list, but I also wanted to know what to expect. "Luckily, we have a lot of hands on deck. What's after that?"

"Build the gate. Prepare the way with the blood of the guilty."

My turn to blink. "Seriously?"

"That's what it says."

Gates, I knew a lot about. Blood, not so much. "Does it say whose blood?"

The Singer shook her head. "Just that they have to be guilty of something. Weird, isn't it? Usually it's the blood of the innocent."

Mr. Landon let out a shaky breath. "I really don't like this."

"Neither do we," Burns said. "Going ahead with this spell tips the balance of things further. It makes things more dangerous for the people in the Faery realm. If the demon is summoned and not defeated, we could end up in the same circumstances as before. There will be war. Atrocities. No way out."

Malek snapped his fingers. Got everyone's attention. He signed.

Kevin spoke the words out loud for those of us who didn't know ASL. "You got another suggestion?"

Burns frowned. "Unfortunately, not."

"Then stop wasting time," Kevin translated. "If it was up to me, I'd have killed the stupid bitch and been done with it. If I'd done that, we'd never know what she did or how to put things back how they were."

He was admitting that he'd been wrong. I'd wanted him to be wrong, and I'd bet on it. I didn't feel vindicated or puffed up, or even happy. I only felt more worried.

Malek signed again, and Kevin spoke. "I'm here to keep an eye on her. I'm here to help. You cops are smart, you'll do the same."

Reid folded his arms across his chest.

I interrupted whatever he was about to say. "Not all of us like each other. Captain Obvious, reporting for duty. We have a goal. We have a way to get there. What we don't have are choices. Either we do it or we don't. We succeed or we fail. For sure we fail if we sit here arguing about it."

Reid settled down. Looked away from me. "What do you want us to do?"

"I think we have to start with the summoning. That's next. Singer, give us the list of stuff we need to get."

"Blood of the guilty," she said.

"More blood?"

Malek signed. *Blood is life.*

"This just gets better and better, doesn't it? What else?"

The Singer read from the list. "Earth from where the willow tree used to be—living earth. Living fire. Living water. Breath of the Singer. Well, hell."

"That book's old," I said. "Older than you. How can it talk about you like that? Who would've known about you?"

She bit her lip. "I'm not the first Singer, Rude. I'm not even the only Singer, though I'm probably the only one close to here. And by close, I mean in the country, maybe even all of North America. When I die—and I will, even if I go back to being one–hundred-percent faery, because we're really long-lived but not immortal—another one will be born. Who knows if they'll be human or not. Could be a baby girl or a baby boy. But there'll for sure be one."

Amy moved Kevin's hands and leveraged herself upright. "So, you're not that special."

The Singer favored her with a sympathetic smile. "My secret's out."

Amy cocked her head. Not the answer she expected. Then again, I had to remember she hadn't spent that much time around the Singer. She only knew what Kevin told her, which wouldn't have been a lot. Or whatever she made up on her own steam. Amy had a vivid imagination. She'd spun herself a good story about the mysterious, beautiful fae woman who loved her boyfriend.

The Singer took a deep breath. "This basically calls for the magical elements. Earth, air, fire, water, spirit."

"Spirit?" Amy asked.

"The blood. It calls for all of those, enlivened by the soul of this place. The land. The city."

"Powerful stuff," Stacy said solemnly.

The Singer nodded. "This demon is one of the most ancient, the strongest. There are laws in place that keep beings as powerful as he is out of the human world. He can't show up here without an invitation."

"Melody invited him," Stacy said.

"It's not enough. The magical caretakers of this place have to invite him, too. They have to give him the magical elements of this place, and they have to do it freely. Of course, that'll give the demon dominion over everything and everyone here."

Stacy whistled. "We have to do all that to make him real here and kill him?"

The Singer nodded again.

Amy narrowed her eyes. "Why can't we just send him back where he came from?"

"Because that won't return our world to normal. Only killing the demon will do that."

"Even if we return it, it won't be the same," Amy said softly.

Her words stilled the room.

She had to be thinking about her parents and what they'd become. What they'd done. Would they forget when they became human again, or would they remember?

Something in her face made my breath catch in my throat. She wasn't only talking about her parents. She was talking about herself.

I opened my mouth to ask, but before I could Stacy steeled herself and focused us on the mission.

"Then we'd better kill him before he becomes the king of every-thing," she said. "Let's not screw it up."

I met Stacy's gaze. She looked as concerned as I felt.

"We need to gather the ingredients," she said. "Who gets what?"

"The blood's mine," Melody said. "I'll collect it myself."

Malek signed. *Sure you don't want help?*

She met his gaze. "You can watch if that's what gets you off."

I so didn't want to know what got Malek off.

I looked at Kevin. "I can take the earth from the park. I have this feeling the spell's not calling for run-of-the-mill dirt. Which means looking sideways again."

"You should take Scott with. You need someone to watch your back. The safest place for him is with—"

Scott broke in. "—with somebody who has superpowers, because I'm power-free."

"No offense, man," Kev said.

"Not much taken. What're you going to do?"

"I can get the river water."

"I could be wrong," I said, "but there's no rivers in the city limits."

"There are bayous."

They served the same purpose as a river would. Catching water from rainfall, streams, and creeks. Carrying it out to sea.

Kevin reached for Amy's hand. "Wanna go with?"

She nodded. And she got that nervous look again.

"Which," Stacy said with a heaping helping of false cheer, "leaves the living fire. Who's up for getting some of that with me?"

Burns and Reid raised their hands. Of course they did. There wasn't anybody else.

Mr. Landon took the last pull from his mug. "I'm the fort. The fort."

We'd covered all the angles. So why did I feel like I was missing something? "Hey, Malek?"

He glanced at me.

"You're staying with Melody, yeah? You and the Singer?"

As long as I can.

"What does that mean?"

Means as long as I can.

Kevin touched my shoulder. Amy fidgeted at his side. "We leaving in the dark?" he asked. "Or do we got time for an hour of shut-eye?"

In spite of the caffeine racing through my veins, the thought of sleep was a siren's song of *Oh God, please.* The room and everyone in it flickered. First they were there, then not there, then back again. My imagination, right?

No. My sight.

I forced words out of my mouth. Forced them to sound as close to normal as I could get them. "I'm worried that if I take the time to do that, I'll wish I hadn't later. I'd rather be early with everything than late. You know?"

He nodded. "That's one side of the coin."

"What's the other?"

"The thing you're not telling me. You worried that if you fall asleep, you'll wake up all Destroyer?"

"Maybe." I glanced at Scott as he made his way over to us. "Hey, can you drive? I can't see straight."

Scott nodded. "S.l.e.e.p."

"No," I said. "I literally can't see straight."

I felt like I'd had too much to drink and been put to bed only to watch the ceiling spin.

Then, the flickering sped up. Instead of people in flesh-and-blood bodies, I saw only the colors. Only the light and darkness.

Malek, black and moody. The cops, green like growing things—the kind with thorns. Stacy was the deep blue sea. And Scott was a solid, got-my-back brown.

"The change?" Scott asked.

Change: Six letters. One syllable. One monster. "I'm pretty sure that my operating a motor vehicle isn't in anybody's best interests right now."

Kevin, radiating a dance club-worthy strobe of white light, nodded. "Scott, you might not have magic, but you've got common sense. Your gut tells you something's about to happen, you listen to it. You figure Rude's about to lose his shit, knock him out."

"Then what? Throw him over my shoulder? Lock him in the trunk —oh, wait, the Explorer doesn't have one of those. Drive him where before he wakes up?"

"Here," Kevin said.

"Your dad will be able to do what, exactly?"

The Singer stepped in, resting both hands on Kev's shoulders. I expected him to tense up, but he relaxed at her touch.

"Leave the problem to me," she said.

Mr. Landon set down his mug. "Everyone's got a plan. That's great. But no one is going anywhere without breakfast."

I started to protest that we didn't have time to eat. Then I realized that I had a hollow where my stomach used to be.

Mr. Landon set down his mug. "Scott, make another pot. Kevin, get the eggs and bacon from the fridge. Everybody else, out."

We stared at him.

He stared back. Waved his arms. "Now."

I walked with everyone else into the living room and then slipped down the hall to the bathroom. I locked the door behind me and leaned on it for a few minutes in the dark, breathing in the ghosts of mint toothpaste and spray deodorant.

The room had one window, high up on the far wall, the bottom frosted and the top clear. I could see the moon through the clear glass, huge and round and bright and not quite full. It would be full tomorrow night, though.

I reached up to my left and flipped the switch. The overhead light and the Hollywood bulbs around the mirror flickered on. Kev and his dad had an ocean blue thing going on. Shower curtain, floor mat, tile, towels. Even the squirt bottle for the antibacterial soap. The toilet seat had been left in the no-women-live-here position. I was looking at everything else because I didn't want to look at myself.

It was easier to pretend I could work the problem and keep my shit together if I didn't. I knew better. If I kept pretending to be who everyone thought I was—who I'd convinced myself I was—I'd screw up at a crucial moment. Oscar had been telling me that for the last year, at first in easy-to-ignore, subtle ways, then in outright, unflinching words the night he'd sent me to the oak portal outside the Rollins Pub.

And now Oscar was gone, maybe forever.

I braced my hands on the edge of the counter and made myself gaze at my own reflection.

People had definitely been telling me the truth about my looks. Black eyes, including the used-to-be-whites—that, I'd already seen for myself. But the color of my skin, how pale it was. The way my orange hair had bleached white. I looked like a vampire, and not the romantic, movie star kind.

I glanced down at my hands. What next? Long, sharp nails? Death rays that shot out of my fingertips?

I looked myself in the eye. Checked around my head for the same colors I'd seen in and around everyone else. There was nothing there. Not good news nothing. More like extremely bad news. In my case, we were talking empty space where there should be something. A void. A giant sucking sound.

Demon. Destroyer.

Would I leave a wreckage in my wake? The city already had plenty of that. Given how many people had disappeared when Melody flash-banged, I was more than a little surprised that the whole place hadn't disappeared with them.

Maybe that was my job.

Instead of smashing up what she'd left, I made it vanish. Like it'd never been in the first place. Millions of lives snuffed out. Miles and miles of houses and offices and stores and parks, gone in a puff of smoke. The only things left? Melody and her demon. And me.

I'd started working with Oscar what felt like a million years ago. He never asked me to take any oaths. Never made me promise anything. He'd taught me what he knew. I studied. He handed out orders. I followed them.

Most of the time, stuff went the way he said it would. Occasionally, everything went pear-shaped and I had to improvise. I did okay. Sometimes I came out bloody, but the job always got done. I always saved the day. Or at least I helped.

The stuff Melody said to me about being a hero? I could pretend it was bullshit. Who did I think I was fooling? I'd done the hero thing for years. I did it like breathing and walking and talking and brushing my teeth.

I had unheroic parts. Qualities I ignored, that made me feel ashamed.

I could still hero on, but for how long? When would the tide turn? Would I go blind? Would I stop feeling love for my friends? Would I stop knowing the right thing to do? Or would I know it, but not care? Would I know right and do wrong in spite of it?

The thought made my balls shrink to the size of raisins. My skin felt paper-thin. Raw. Like all my nerves had clawed their way to the surface.

My stomach rolled over. Acid rushed into my throat. I bent over the sink and threw up the coffee I'd swallowed, and then some bile after that. I gave myself a couple of minutes to see if my stomach had anything else to vomit before I turned on the tap to clean the sink, splash cold water on my face, and rinse out my mouth.

Somebody knocked on the door.

I pulled myself together. "I'll be right out."

"I just want to come in." Melody.

I wiped my mouth with the back of my hand. Turned the lock and opened the door. "I'm not sure you want to be around me."

"Because I fucked up your life?"

"You don't think that's a good reason?"

"No, it's great. I just need to talk to you. Please."

I had a deep-seated feeling I'd regret it, but I stepped out of her way. She slipped past me, closed the toilet seat and the cover, and plopped down on it. "You've got to keep Malek away from me."

I had an easy answer for that one. "No."

"But—"

"No, Melody."

She shifted on her seat. "I know I've played a little fast and loose with the truth."

"That's all it takes."

"No second chance?"

"You're delusional."

She sighed. "What did you come in here for anyway? Couldn't be the ambience."

"Time alone. And you know, to pee."

"Yeah, this is probably the only room in the house where you'll find it the alone time. And, like, the toilet. But you can't stay in here all night, you know. Other people will have to pee."

I leaned against the wall. "This is why you wanted to talk to me?"

"I just suck at getting to the point."

I waited.

She pushed to her feet. "It's bad, isn't it? I wish it didn't have to be that way for you."

A roundhouse full of pity. "What are you talking about?"

"Discovering you're evil."

"Who're you talking about, Melody? I'm not evil."

"You, Rude Davies. You're a good guy turning bad from the inside out."

"This is happening to me because of your spell. You did this."

She shoved her hands into the pockets of her overalls. "I didn't plan how the magic would affect people. What's happening to you, it's because of who you are on the inside. I know because that's how it happened with me. The super hot flashes and melting down trash cans and car parts. Finding the stuff in my mom's diary about my dad and finally understanding why. I fought it, Rude. Teeth, claws —everything."

"It didn't work, did it? Fighting."

"Nothing I did made any difference. Not even a little. I finally had to give in."

I smacked the back of my head into the wall. "What did that feel like?"

"A lot better, like a weight lifted off me. I started to notice small things. The way things made me angry. The raw deal I'd gotten from people who were supposed to be my family. The whispers at school. The way people trip me in the halls. How much they hate me. I figured out how to use all that, how to be myself and stop pretending to be someone else. I stopped pretending to be better."

"What are you trying to say, Melody?"

"That this hero thing you've got going on doesn't make up for the way your parents don't notice you or how you're carrying a responsibility on your shoulders that's way too big. It doesn't make up for all your frustration and how you're pissed off and you have no life besides what your teacher tells you to have."

"Thanks for pointing that out. Nice touch about my parents."

She took another step toward me. One more foot forward and she'd be on top of me. "You think that's a secret?"

"Well, yeah."

"It's not hard to see if you have eyes. Especially for people like us."

People with what?—unsatisfactory home lives? Mine had its share of awful, but Melody's won by a mile in the crap category. So, she noticed. So what?

"You really think I've got all this potential for destruction in me. That it goes deep enough to change my outside, too. That I should give into it."

She shook her head. "I'm just saying I know what it feels like to become the thing you've always feared."

I looked at her. She wasn't trying to hurt me. She was trying to help in her own strange way. "How can you fear becoming something you didn't even believe existed? You didn't know about demons before."

"Sure I did," she said. "I knew my stepfather."

No sulfur or fire or brimstone involved. Except in every other way, it was completely the same.

She took that last step. I smelled the coffee on her breath. Felt an electric charge flowing off her. The hairs on my arms stood tall. She rose up on her toes and wrapped her arms around my neck. I froze like an idiot. I half-hugged her back.

The curve of her breasts pressed against my chest sent all my senses into high gear. Especially the new ones that told me the color around her heart had softened to a rosy pink.

"You're welcome." She kissed my cheek. Pulled away with a shy smile on her lips.

I didn't want to believe that she could be shy. Or tender. I watched her open the door and head out. She threw a glance over her shoulder with a question written on her face.

You coming?

I looked in the mirror. Saw nothing in my reflection that wasn't already inside of me. Nothing I could do anything about. No reason to stay.

Melody had disappeared from the hall, leaving only me and the former god who waited for me. He blocked my path. He narrowed his eyes and studied mine.

"What's up, Malek?"

Watch yourself.

"Trust me, I am."

He shook his head. *You're falling.*

"Into what?"

Stupidity.

"I have no idea what you're talking about."

I'm talking about Melody. She's taking you in.

"There's nothing to take."

Only your soul.

So far, I'd seen her lie like a boss. I'd seen her magic out of control. I'd also seen her vulnerable as hell. She understood what I was going through. I noticed her body. Who wouldn't? I might be half-monster, but I wasn't dead.

She just wanted to belong somewhere. To someone. She wanted to be loved.

Everything she'd ever known about herself had been slashed to ribbons the instant she found out about her real father. She'd done stuff she never would've dreamed of before because her demon blood gave her the power to get what she needed. She thought she could control it, but she couldn't. In the end, it could destroy her. It could destroy everyone and everything around her.

I understood. I wished I didn't.

I held Malek's gaze. "I have no intention of doing anything I shouldn't."

I'm calling it like I see it.

"Thanks," I said, "but I'm the seer here."

Not anymore. You're something else. You're on the edge.

He stared at me so hard my feet wanted to backpedal.

I held my ground—barely. "The edge of what?"

His eyes filled with sadness. *The point of no return.*

"I don't feel like it."

You won't. It'll feel normal to you.

"That scares me worse than anything."

I know. That's what makes you who you are.

"So what do I do?"

Watch out for yourself the best you can. I'll help you if I can.

"Thanks," I said. What he'd said reminded me of another conversation. "Malek, you knew I was there in the shop when you were with Amy, right?"

He nodded.

"What did you do to her?"

That's for her to tell.

"She hasn't breathed a word about it. And Kevin's taking her to get the water. It'll just be the two of them. Is there something he needs to know?"

Watch out for her.

Malek turned on his heel and walked away.

CHAPTER 9

MR. LANDON DIDN'T have enough eggs in the house to feed so many people, so breakfast ended up part eggs and part browned ground beef, sliced green apples, spinach salad, and watered-down orange juice. The scrape of forks on plates and the occasional burp took the place of conversation.

I made an extra plate for Zach. He ate hugely. Mr. Landon figured he could find a bag of kibble in one of the neighbor's empty houses—one bright spot in a world of shadow. I tried to hold onto that, but worry invaded.

Even if the group split up to make gathering the necessary items go faster, we had too much to do and, by my calculations, barely enough time. Not to mention the arrival of the demon in the home stretch and what the hell to do after that. And that was if things played out like we planned. When had that ever happened?

We didn't have working phones. We couldn't keep in touch with each other after we went our separate ways. If anything else went sideways for any one of us, that meant the end. Didn't it?

If we couldn't complete the spell, then we had no chance to restore the city and everyone in it. We'd slide into some kind of apocalyptic devolution, and we wouldn't even know it until too late.

Seer's magic might be able to connect us with one another. It'd be a big spell, though, and beyond my power to do. I needed help, and, with all the magic in the room, only one other person had the right skill set.

I crooked my finger at Stacy as soon as she shoveled the last bite of spinach into her mouth. She chewed while we wove through the crowd and the laundry room to the back door with its single bare window. The dog followed us, but stopped short of bounding outside. I'd never known a dog not to want to go outside unless it rained, but Zach stood on his hind legs to watch us through the glass after we stepped onto the patio.

"Kevin's dad let the yard go, didn't he?" Stacy asked. "Or maybe it was Melody's spell."

Where the patio ended, knee-high grass full of dandelions took over. A trio of old, tall pines stood guard near the back fence, crows brooding in the branches. The branches of the solitary oak in the center of the yard held even more of the birds, its branches seeming to bowing under their weight. The crows studied me as if I were a lab specimen.

"What do you think about that?" I asked.

"I'm wondering whether they understand what we're saying."

"Really? And I just thought it was creepy."

"Sarcasm. Nice. They're listening, you know."

"There's got to be a reason they're showing up everywhere. Are they listening for themselves or on behalf of someone else?"

"I don't sense any connection that would tell me another person is working them."

I looked at her. "You can tell just like that? No spell? No trance?"

"Yeah. It's my thing."

For her, the natural world was not only alive, it had consciousness she could sense. Every kind of being from bees to trees had a job to do, work that kept the world turning on its axis. For her, every living thing was a face of God, or the Goddess, or whatever you wanted to call the divine.

"What do you think they want?"

"Well, we have major mojo in the house, Rude. That attracts attention. But you've been seeing them other places?"

"Ever since all this started."

"Then it's you. You're the reason. So the question is, what do they want from you?"

"No idea."

"Grackles are smart bastards. Corvids—that's what kind of birds they are. Same as crows and rooks and ravens and blue jays. They remember faces, use tools. They learn and teach their kids. They'd make bad enemies and excellent friends."

I hadn't thought about it that way. I hadn't thought about it at all except for how freaked out I felt seeing them everywhere.

"They're fae, you know, one claw in this world and one claw in the other."

I blinked at her.

I should've known that. Maybe once upon a time I had, but I didn't remember. Anxiety rippled through my chest, stealing my air. Ice slicked the surface of my skin, wet and smoking in the heat, chilling me to the bone. The cold wiped every thought from my mind until it felt still and empty and numb. I could barely move. I could barely breathe.

"Deep breaths, Rude."

I couldn't shake my head. Couldn't open my mouth to tell her no.

I closed my eyes, following instinct and intuition, willing my seer's magic to rise, to fight. No answer. Not even a spark of power.

Stacy reached for my back, pressing her palm against the spot between my shoulder blades. One eternal, breathless and terrifying moment later, my panic vanished. One second there, one second gone, just like that. I inhaled deeply, shuddering. A tremor started in the depths of my belly, spreading like wildfire to all my limbs. I shook from the inside out. I couldn't make it stop.

"Breathe again."

I latched on to her voice and did what she asked, head clearing a little more with each inhalation until I managed to croak a single word.

"How?"

"All I did was ground, Rude—connect my body to the earth. Because I was touching you when I did it, I grounded you, too. Do you feel the connection?"

My feet felt heavy, the soles of my sneakers hugging the concrete. My bones felt heavy, too, as if they'd suddenly become aware of gravity. I met her gaze and she met mine, solid and steady. We could've been the only two people in the world, space and time paused and waiting for us to break the moment, to move on.

"I'm here," I said.

"That's called being present, dude."

I flashed a nervous grin.

"I'm going to take my hand away now, okay?"

I nodded.

She lifted her hand. When the world didn't turn pear-shaped, I blew out a long breath and my shoulders dropped from around my ears to their normal height. I glance down at my own hands, at my arms. They were wet.

It hadn't been my imagination. Actual ice had appeared on the surface of my skin from out of nowhere, and as Stacy had grounded me, it'd melted.

Not from nowhere.

The thought flickered across my mind, but didn't feel as if it'd come from inside of me.

"You say something?" I asked.

Stacy shook her head.

I glanced at the crows.

Stacy followed my lead. "They talking to you?"

"Maybe. That's why I wanted to talk with you out here, though."

She furrowed her brow.

"Not because of the birds. Because we need a way to communicate with each other while we're split up. I can't do that magic."

"But I can."

I nodded.

She tucked her curls behind her ears. "I could do something like that, sure. But I can only do it one to one. I could build a connection between, say, you and Kevin. You'd be able to check in with him and vice versa, but that's it. Unless—"

I raised a brow.

She watched the crows. "You'll have to chill out about the birds."

Why would I need to—oh. "What do we need them for?"

"They're going to be our messengers."

"And how are you gonna convince them they want to do that?"

"I'm going to ask politely."

I couldn't picture it, but I wasn't the witch here. She was, and she seemed sure about this.

"I'll need your help. Need to borrow some magic."

"You sure you want mine right now?"

She rolled her eyes. "We use what we've got until it's gone."

I met her gaze and saw no doubt, and no front, either. She trusted me. She believed in me. "So, how do we do this?"

"If we combine our magic—all of us who have magic—and use our connections with each other the right way, we could maybe design a magical network, one where we can communicate mind-to-mind."

"We can do all that? I had hopes for something more, I don't know, fundamental. But if we can get that fancy, that would be amazing."

"I said maybe. It's outside-the-box magic, Rude. I've never tried something like that before, and I've never heard or read about it being done before."

"You're innovating."

"I'm throwing shit against the wall to see if it'll stick."

I shook my head. "You're brilliant, Stace."

"Your magic is key, Rude. You're the magical authority here."

"I keep telling people I'm an apprentice. I'm not an authority."

"You're what we have. You understand what means? We need you. Not the demon or destroyer inside you, whatever it is. You, Rude."

I glanced at my shoes, scuffing one toe against the concrete. "The change that's happening to me, it doesn't matter how I try to stop it."

"It'll happen anyway," she said.

"It's not a matter of if I go bad, Stace. It's a matter of when. I can hope it's not at a crucial moment, but I can't predict anything. I don't want to let all of you down. I don't want to make things worse."

She held my gaze. Behind her, the velvet sky began to lighten to indigo, inviting the dawn. "I trust you."

"Maybe you shouldn't."

"That's why I trust you."

"I don't get it."

"You have a healthy understanding of your limits."

"I don't have any such thing, but it's nice of you to say so."

"I'm not that nice."

Nice could be true, but it could just as easily be patronizing, or it could be a friendly lie. "Kind, then."

She winked at me. "We should do this now."

I nodded.

With a swish of her skirt, she headed inside to gather the others, leaving me alone with the crows. They watched me with more than curiosity. They eyed me with expectation, then with irritation, and, finally, outright annoyance.

"What?"

No response.

The back door opened again—Stacy returning with the Singer, Malek, and Kevin.

"Who's watching Melody?" I asked.

Kevin "Dad, Scott, and Beth."

"All the people without magic." All the people who could get hurt the worst if Melody wanted to harm them.

"No worries. The Singer and I froze her magic and tied her to a chair."

With their magic in flux, how solid could the binding be? Then again, none of us were in good magical shape, and what Kev and the Singer had managed would have to do.

An arrow of pain shot through my forehead. I pressed the heel of my hand to the spot.

"You all right?" Kev asked.

"No, dude."

He frowned.

The Singer glanced at the birds, then looked at Stacy. "We should be under the oak, yeah?"

"We should. Rude should sit with his back against the bark." Stacy stepped into the grass.

The Singer strode after her and tripped over her own feet in a very human manner. My mouth fell open.

Move, Malek signed.

"But she—" I bit off what I'd been about to say. I'd spent so much time thinking about my own change. I wasn't the only one going through a radical reordering of my everything.

How long before the Singer lost the faery magic that augmented her voice? How long before she was just a girl with a very unusual ability to move people when she sang?

I went where Malek pointed and sat down in front of the oak. The grass tickled my legs and stuck up inside my cargo shorts. My luck, I'd sat on a fire ant bed and would spend the rest of the operation numbed on Ibuprofen and covered in a thick, pink layer of calamine lotion. I waited for the stinging to begin. I *wanted* it to begin.

I wanted out of the backyard, away from my friends. I wanted to run from what had happened to my city, from my change and everyone else's, until it was finished. Until I was something else. Something new—

Holy fuck. I would never think those things. Except I had. I was.

Malek stared at me. I held his gaze, cheeks flushing with an unfamiliar feeling. Shame.

"What's going on?" the Singer asked.

I needed to keep my mouth shut. If I breathed so much as a word, she'd learn how I felt. She'd know everything.

She kicked me in the shin.

I grunted.

That sound was all she needed to read me. "His demon nature is beginning to take over."

Stacy shrugged.

The Singer beetled her brow. "He's unstable."

"We're all unstable."

"You're not," the Singer said.

Stacy sighed. "I'm having—I don't know—call them power surges. I don't seem to be turning into anything evil or losing my power, but that's the best I can say."

"Wait," I said. "Why not?"

"Pretty sure it's luck, Rude. And probably because my ancestors are protecting me."

I didn't understand that totally, but I knew she came from a long line of witches, whether they called themselves witches or not.

"Whatever it is, I'm glad," I said.

Her lips quirked into a half-grin. "Lean back, Rude."

The oak's trunk scratched my skin through the cotton of my shirt. I tried to ignore the discomfort, letting my weight sink into the bark and into the ground while the others squatted nearby for a magical chat. I couldn't hear what they said, only the soothing murmur of their voices.

My eyes closed of their own volition. The speed with which my consciousness began to drift surprised me, but not enough to break the undertow of sleep deprivation. I hadn't slept in so long. Sleep would make it all better, steal me away from mounting anxiety and strange thoughts and vampire-pale skin and black eyes and—

Stacy's hand cracked against my cheek.

I blinked at her.

"We talked about this. I need you to be here."

"What?"

"You, Rude. Faery seer, super lucky, all-around badass. Not your inner demon."

"I'll try."

"Don't try. Do it."

I shook my head to clear it.

She narrowed her eyes. "Can you follow your intuition without falling asleep? We need you to focus."

"I hope so."

"Know so."

I nodded once. Forcefully.

She didn't seem satisfied, but she stepped back from me, continuing to increase the distance between us until she came to the outermost edge of the oak's canopy. Although she was only a few feet away, she felt far. Wind kicked up, rocking the branches, alternately covering her in shadow and casting her into light. When the sun shone on her, her hair looked like spun gold, like something out of a fairy tale.

The Singer, Kevin, and Malek moved to stand with her. They held hands for a moment and something I couldn't quite see passed between them—the rise and fall of breath, a pulse of intention, a spark of magic. The fact that I couldn't tell what it was scared me. The fine hairs on my arms rose, making me shiver.

When they let go of each others' hands, I exhaled a shuddering breath. When the Singer began to walk along the edge of the canopy to Stacy's right and my left, the barometric pressure dropped, just like before a thunderstorm. A wave of pain threaded through my sinuses. I gritted my teeth against it until it suddenly stopped, when the Singer halted. Without turning my head, I could barely see her from the corner of my left eye. I didn't want to look at her.

Kevin and Malek walked the opposite direction, Kevin slowing to a stop at my right. A wave of crickets hidden in the grass on the other side of the yard jumped, running for their lives. The thump of their bodies and the spike of their song slid into me, making my skin itch. I tried to fidget where I sat, but my body felt frozen. I could only breathe and blink.

Malek kept moving, the faint whisper of his steps winding behind me. I didn't have to see him to know that when he stopped, his position mirrored Stacy's. I felt the energy between them lock into place. The rumble of thunder shook the air. A faraway flash of lightning spidered through the sky.

The four of them had created a circle around me, each of them guarding a quarter. The paths between Malek and Stacy, and the Singer and Kevin, created a crossroads with me at the center.

The crows screeched overhead, claws clipping at the oak's branches.

Stacy, the Singer, and Kevin took one long step toward me. I imagined that Malek did the same. A flash of blue energy rose from the grass inside the circle, dancing like flames.

They took a second long step. The blue fire grew darker, the flames higher.

One more step in unison, and the blue fire crackled to lightning, darkening to a deep indigo, the color of Stacy's magic. She clapped her hands and the blue lightning shaped itself into a sphere, surrounding us all—humans, tree, birds. A hush descended, stilling the air, the crows, the sound of my breath, the beat of my heart, the rush of my blood. As if time had stopped.

I closed my eyes, willing myself not to sleep, not to run from the one job that mattered right here and now. To dive deep into my seer's intuition.

What remained of my intuition was a horror that stole my breath.

CHAPTER 10

MY INTUITION WAS DARK FIRE, infected with a demon's power. Still on a leash, still mine to control, but it had a mind of its own and so much feeling, the emotion bottled up and blocked like lava and steam beneath solid rock.

Frustration. Rage.

They wanted to break free. They *needed* to lose control, to tear down the trees and the birds and my friends, and everything beyond that. They wouldn't stop until the streets ran red with blood.

More than that, they wanted to un-make everything living thing in the vicinity. To wipe it all completely from the world. I smelled shredded earth and tasted burnt flesh.

It was only a matter of time before the demon inside me broke free. It was stronger than me. It was made for this new dystopia. It belonged here.

A vision bloomed in my mind: an empty city, streets gone to rubble, windows smashed, the air reeking of oil and fire, the wind hellish. Rusted metal. Strangled weeds. Bones picked clean. It was more than an empty city—it was an empty world. Not because of Melody.

Because of me.

The voice of my inner demon shook me to the core, trembling my bones and turning the blood in my veins molten.

Look at me.

Just three small words. Three punches to the gut.

I tried to speak, but words refused to obey my will. I tried to turn my gaze away, but I couldn't move. I could only stare at the face it showed me.

Not the ghost-white skin and black, pupil-less eyes I expected to see, but the fearful face of a little boy who had no safe home. Hair the color of the setting sun and long enough to fall into his eyes. Spindly arms and legs. Long feet punched into scuffed white sneakers, the rest of his skinny body wrapped in a pair of khaki shorts that dusted the tops of his shins and a grass-stained white T-shirt with the Houston Astros logo splashed across the front.

The demon showed me my own reflection.

I shook my head, not getting it—not wanting to understand.

I'd worn that shirt and those shorts a hundred times the year I turned seven. The particular pattern of grass stains and the specific scuffs of my shoes pointed to a certain day, every detail seared into my brain. No, it was deeper than that. The memory branded my soul.

Riding my bike one block over, hands at my sides, steering with subtle shifts of weight as the noon sun baked the asphalt, I'd felt enchanted by the feeling of freedom. Out there, all alone, I was perfect. If I lost control of the bike and went over, no one yelled. I could wave at neighbors without worry about the neighborhood politics between them and my parents. I could laugh at something without wondering whether laughing was the right thing.

If the freedom was fragile, like a glass that had been dropped too many times, cracks running its length but not breaking it—not yet. I treated it like the treasure it was.

That day, the grassy esplanade that divided the block between north and south seemed to catch fire, only the fire was the wrong color, a true and loud green I'd never seen before. It called to something in me, and the call felt so strong, I rode into the grass before it occurred to me that the green fire might be dangerous.

It climbed the tires and the aluminum frame of my bike, wound like a vine from the soles of my sneakers to my thighs, dancing along my skin. It didn't hurt me.

After that, I saw the green fire everywhere I went, anywhere trees and grass and plants grew. I understood instinctively that the fire was some kind of magic and that no one else saw it. That was cool, because the fire and I shared a secret. And we were friends.

It was my only friend.

My troubled child self stared into the eyes of my troubled older self, pleading to be released.

I began to shake, the uncontrollable tremor starting in my bones and working outward until my fingers and arms and legs trembled.

Please, the child-demon said.

It took every ounce of will to shake my head. To back away from the demon.

I gave you the thing you needed most, and you hate me for it.

The truth in those words stunned. Slowly, mercilessly, the truth cracked open my heart. It hurt so much, it stunned me still and silent.

I didn't know how to answer the demon—the little boy who had no safe home. I didn't even know how to try.

I turned away, grabbing hold of the dark fire inside me and any shreds of intuition it might hold, using its power to launch my consciousness and my magic into the air, into the branches of the tree where the crows waited.

I spoke the question I'd come to ask.

They answered with a rush of wings.

The vision ended suddenly and violently, slamming my consciousness back into my body like a hammer smashing a nail. I couldn't breathe. I couldn't move. Panic bloomed in the bowl of my belly, clawing up the long trail of my spine into my throat.

The demon's voice slip-slid into my waking mind.

Please.

My head rocked to the side once. Twice. I felt the air moving before a third blow. Grabbed whatever had been about to hit me again. Forced my eyes open.

I gripped Stacy's arm at the wrist, fingers dug into her skin.

Her words seemed to come from a hundred miles away. They echoed inside my head. "Rude, are you all right?"

I shook my head.

"Can you let go of me?"

I did what she asked. My cheeks heated when I saw I'd left marks on her.

She studied my face. "The magic worked. I felt it. But something happened to you."

It took a long moment to conjure words, to make my mouth move properly. "It was just a memory."

"Of?"

"The first day I encountered magic."

"Why would that come up now?"

"That's the day my demon was born."

She shook her head—not at me, but at the others, who'd started to move in closer. They glanced at each other, then took several steps back, voices low as they talked with one another. Kevin ignored her directive. He made his way to us and joined Stacy as she sat in the grass beside me.

"Tell us."

If I told the story out loud, that would make it more real. It would take a ghost and turn it into flesh and blood, and I one-hundred-percent could not do that. "No."

She took a deep breath and started again. "Maybe it will help if you let it out."

"If I let it out, the world ends. I saw it in my vision. Empty streets, broken glass, bones everywhere."

"Talking about a memory isn't the same as releasing the demon."

"How do you know?"

She turned over the question in her mind. "Okay, I'll drop it for now, not forever."

I'd take what I could get.

Kevin shook his head. "I'm not ready to let it go."

"Too bad."

"You've been terrified of what's happening to you, Rude. I thought you were worried about turning into the thing you fight every day, but it's deeper than that. More personal. Something happened to you."

I stared at him. "And you think you understand because your mom died."

"I'm not gonna pretend I can stand in your shoes," he said. "But I know what it's like to have your whole world turned upside down. To have to deal with more than anyone should ever have to handle."

"You're my friend."

He nodded.

"Once upon a time, I didn't have any friends. No human ones, anyway."

He mulled that. "That why you try so hard to be everyone's friend now? Why you're always the life of the party?"

I laughed. "Twist the knife."

"Didn't know I'd stabbed you."

I met his gaze. "Kev, I don't want to talk about it."

"You need to."

"Please," I said, struck by how closely my plea resembled my begging inner demon's.

He held up both hands in a gesture of surrender.

The relief I felt was so strong, I could've cried.

Stacy leaned towards me, nudging my leg with her knee. She wanted me to know I wasn't alone, that she had my back. She said something I didn't hear, or couldn't process the meaning of.

"What?" I asked.

"The spell worked."

Incredibly well, all things considered. "The crows will watch for us. They'll report in if they see anything demonically alarming, and they'll act as conduits for us if and when our changing magic erodes the spell of connection. And it's not just the crows here in the yard—they'll tell their friends. We have their whole network."

Stacy nodded. "That's what I think, too."

Good that she agreed. It helped draw me a little closer to calm.

Kevin rubbed his hands together. "We've done everything we can do here. We should get moving."

The way he said *we,* it sounded as if he meant everyone except me. "Kev—"

"You should stay here, Rude."

"Absolutely not."

"How's the balance in you—the one between human and demon?"

I didn't have to look inside to check. The demon had been rising before the spell. Now it was all I could do to keep it locked down.

Kevin read all of that on my face. "You've got what—one more shot of big magic in you before you turn all the way?"

I didn't want to admit that to myself, much less to him. But this was bigger than me. Larger than the morass of bad, hard feelings brewing in my chest. I couldn't get a handle on them. I couldn't even name them all.

I drew a shaky breath. "Sounds about right."

"Stay here. We got this."

That went against everything I'd tried to become my whole life to sit on the sidelines. It went against all of my magical training. And he was right. If I were in his shoes, I'd have said the same thing.

Kevin looked me in the eye. "Do you trust me?"

"Yes." The word tasted like ashes in my mouth, but it was the truth. I'd never trusted anyone more.

"Malek will go in your place."

"Scott's gonna love that."

"Scott will do whatever we need him to do. We'll be back soon. Then we'll all go together to stop Melody's dad. Okay?"

I nodded.

He and Stacy pushed to their feet, then reached down to help me up. My legs trembled, but they held me. I'd never felt so tired in my entire life, and I could eat a horse on top of the enormous breakfast I'd put away.

"Dad will fix you something," Kevin said.

I looked at him sideways.

"Your stomach's growling, man."

I hadn't noticed. "I know where your peanut butter cup stash is."

He flashed a wry grin.

The first golden fingers of dawn brushed the sky as we closed the door behind us. I didn't like it. It felt too bright, like a spotlight.

Melody sat in Mr. Landon's kitchen chair, rope bisecting her clothes and skin. She met my gaze and held it. I read sorrow in her eyes, and tenderness, understanding. Not love, but something like it.

I turned and caught a glimpse of myself in the curved black mirror of the dead TV screen. I looked like warmed-over dog crap. Besides the monster mash, I had a cut lip and a set of black-and-blues. My forehead. Side of my head. No recollection of having been hit.

A pit of despair opened inside my chest.

On the way to his room, Kevin waved for me to follow. Once we'd crossed the threshold, he opened the dresser drawer that held his candy stash.

"You know what to do," he said.

I did. The chocolate and peanut butter helped a little with the ache inside, and right now a little was everything. I tried to put on a good face, to concentrate on strategy. Anything except my own raging problem. "Which bayou are you and Amy going to for the water?"

He blew out a shaky breath. "Buffalo."

"Not the closest to here."

"No, but it is closest to the heart of the city. It feels right."

I couldn't argue with that. "I'll be keeping track of you. You need something, don't hesitate to ask."

"I won't. I mean it."

I believed him.

He changed his clothes while I ate, then sat beside me and pulled on clean socks. Slipped his feet into his sneakers. "Amy's still mum about what happened at Malek's. I told her I knew he'd done magic for her. That he'd given her a tat. She refused to show it to me. Can you believe that?"

"No. Yes." I shook my head. "She's not right, Kevin. You get that, don't you? There's all this emotion underneath her surface. It's as if she can barely hold it in. Barely keep it together."

"She's been through a lot," he said.

"Maybe she doesn't have the same kind of coping skills we have."

"Or maybe she just feels things more than the rest of us."

"That's power," I said.

He looked at me. "How do you mean?"

"She always talks about how she doesn't have superpowers, but being able to feel that much, that's—I don't know what that is. But it feels like something."

"I wouldn't wish it on my worst enemy."

I tried to imagine what it must be like for her. My imagination agreed with Kev. "Maybe I'm talking out of my ass. It's probably nothing."

"Never is."

"Just be careful. Both of you."

"Will do. Why don't you sack out in here?"

"I don't see how I can if I have to watch Melody."

"The Singer is staying, too. She can watch while you're out."

"You've got it all figured out."

"I wish. Amy and I are catching a ride with Scott and Malek. That ought to be a blast."

"Yeah. Thanks, dude."

"No problem. Just don't get any crumbs in my bed." He rooted through his dirty jeans pockets. Grabbed his wallet and his phone.

"Phones still don't work."

"Neither does my money." He shoved them in his pockets anyway. "Habit. Still feels weird, this no shirt thing."

"Wings in the way."

"Yeah." Kevin rubbed the bridge of his nose. "Don't worry, Rude. Not about me, and not about the rest of us. I told you that we got this. I need you to believe that."

"I do." I said it automatically, but I meant it.

He looked at me—no, he looked into me, gauging the truth in my words. You couldn't lie to the fae. They always knew.

Satisfied, he squared his shoulders. "See you later."

I listened as his footfalls faded down the hall. Heard the front door open and remain open as my friends headed out to get what we needed. I trusted them to gather the stuff we needed. The worry was for the missing and the monsters, for the pain and death that would come for us all if we couldn't return to the ways things were.

I worried for myself. What if I was the reason we screwed it all up? What if I changed completely at some crucial moment? What if my friends had to fight not only Melody's demon, but mine?

Zach jumped onto the bed and curled up at my side. His warmth and his trust in spite of what I was becoming—and how much worse it could get—was everything.

I laid down, exhaustion weighing my limbs, forcing my eyes closed. The last sound I heard was the Explorer's engine gunning to life and the squeal of its brakes as Scott pulled out of the driveway. Sleep took me deep.

I dreamed about my friends, as if I was looking down on them from above. As if I had a bird's eye view.

Stacy and the faery cops in the woods. Correction, swampy woods that smelled of mud and water shaded by four different kinds of oak trees, pecan trees, bald cypress. There was a lake, and there were alligators.

They were southwest of Houston, at Brazos Bend State Park.

Stacy hunkered on the shore looking for something among the rocks, fingertips brushing the dirt, picking up small stones and discarding them one by one. What she was after, I didn't know—until I remembered from my scout days that flint could be found near bodies of fresh water, or places that had once been underwater. She had to be searching for flint, and it would have to be taken directly from the land. It couldn't be bought or stolen. Not to make the kind of fire we needed.

Lake water had soaked the hem of her skirt, her sandals, and her feet. She took a squishy step around a mat of twigs and grass and soil. A hissing sound rose close by. Officer Burns stepped between Stace and the source of that sound—a mother gator guarding her nest. All six feet of her.

Any sane person would've backed away, but Burns stood his

ground. He said something to the mama in a language I didn't understand. She didn't retreat, but she didn't charge him, either. Not yet.

Stacy ignored her completely, plucking a stone from the earth. Smooth, gray, and dry. She slid a pocketknife from her skirt pocket and flicked its iron blade open. Struck the stone seven times. On the last blow, the stone sparked.

"Got it," she said.

Officer Reid held a glass jar in one hand and his gun in the other. "Good. We should go."

She shook her head. "Not yet."

"Then at least do us all a favor and move away from the nest, okay?"

"I should make the fire right here."

"You're going to die right here, girl."

"Just hold her off for a few minutes longer, will you? And bring the jar."

He muttered under his breath, but he did what she asked. The jar had a slip of paper inside. With ink marks. A handwritten spell.

Stacy pulled a couple of dry balls of oak moss from her pocket. She went to work with the blade and the flint. Seconds ticked by, and sparks flared, but the moss didn't catch.

The mama gator took a step toward Burns. He matched it. Kept the gator's eyes on him.

Stacy closed her eyes. Spoke a spell or a prayer. I read the words on her lips. *The living fire. We have need. Blessed be the powers of the great Elements. The living fire. The living flame.*

She said it over and over again, striking spark after spark.

The mama gator hissed.

The oak moss caught, burning with bright flame that rapidly heated to blue at its core.

Stacy dropped it in the jar. The fire consumed the moss and the paper in a single flare, and left no ash behind. With all the fuel gone, the flame should've gone out, but it didn't. The oranges and yellows in it faded, leaving the blue—the hottest part of the fire.

Burns kept his gaze on the gator. "Stacy, wrap it up."

She set the jar down for a moment. Replaced her pocketknife. Spoke a blessing over the flint, which she laid gently in the spot where she'd found it. Then she picked up the glass again—from the bottom. The impossible fire didn't seem to burn her hand through the glass.

Stacy held it tightly, retracing her steps without turning around, without taking her gaze off Burns and the alligator. She backpedaled until she'd gone a good thirty feet. Reid followed her closely. Only then did Burns follow in their steps.

The mama gator kept pace with him, continuing to hiss, the strength of the muscle beneath her armor wound up and ready to loose like an arrow.

She lunged.

I sat bolt upright in Kevin's bed, breath hard and fast, heart racing. I opened my thoughts to any message the crows might send, any vision or thought or word. None came.

The Singer appeared in the doorway, her eyes dark. "You up?"

I nodded.

"Did something happen?"

The question hung in the air between us. "You didn't see Stacy and the fae cops at the park?"

"Nothing."

Maybe nothing had happened then. Maybe it had been just a dream. The Singer would know, wouldn't she? The crows would've told her.

I sighed. "How long was I out?"

"Two hours."

"That's too long."

"You needed the shut-eye. We have a problem, though. Melody's gone."

I stared at her. "What? When?"

"While I was watching. And no, I didn't take my eyes off of her. She just disappeared into the air. Vanished."

"She was supposed to wait for us."

"I guess she didn't want us to interfere with gathering the blood of the guilty."

Her mom. Her stepfather. "She left a note behind."

I stood up, knees popping. "Show me."

She handed me a sheet of paper torn from the notepad on Mr. Landon's desk. Melody's handwriting was all loops and squiggles. It made my head hurt.

I have to do this. Don't try to stop me.

CHAPTER 11

I BREATHED IN THE GHOST of bacon grease. Afternoon light slanted through the blinds like spears, piercing the motes that floated in the air. Every nerve in my body seemed to vibrate at once. For a heartbeat, my vision grayed and I felt weightless, then heavy, as if I'd winked out of existence and back again.

Beth sat at the near end of the kitchen table, open spell book in front of her, looking guilty. She stared at Mr. Landon's empty seat, where Melody had been moments before, foam cushion still dented from her weight.

"What did you do?" I asked.

She shook her head. "I swear I didn't help her escape."

"Did you try to stop her?"

Beth frowned. "How?"

"She doesn't have magic, remember?" The Singer wrapped her fingers around the back of the empty chair. "Melody got the jump on both of us."

The Singer had excellent magical reflexes—or she would've, if she weren't becoming human. I should never have fallen asleep. I should never have left them alone with Melody. I should've had another cup of coffee or propped my eyelids open with toothpicks, whatever I needed to do.

"Stop beating yourself up," the Singer said.

"I haven't even gotten going yet."

"You're human, and going through huge changes. Your body, mind, and spirit can only take so much."

"If I'd been here—"

"Maybe it would've made a difference, but maybe not. We'll never know. Focus on now."

She spoke with finality, and with enough traces of power in her voice to make me do what she wanted. I could see the threads of magic as they wrapped around me. I felt them sink into my skin like poisoned barbs. I winced.

"My magic hurts?" she asked.

I nodded.

She pressed her lips into a thin line. She didn't say anything, but I didn't need her to. I knew what her expression meant, how far gone I was.

I sighed. "Where were you when Melody vanished?"

The Singer pointed toward the counter, where she'd sat next to Malek during the pre-dawn meeting. "I was composing the magic we need for the spell against the demon."

Sheets of paper lay next to where she'd been. No musical notes, only penciled-in lyrics.

"She was just talking," the Singer said. "Going on about the classes she takes every day. Living at Beth's house. How crazy Beth's mom is." Her tone dropped half an octave. "How she's such good friends with Amy."

"How uncomfortable for you."

Beth looked up at both of us, eyes huge behind her glasses. "You could cut the tension with a machete."

I sighed. "You know where Melody used to live?"

"We went there with her to pick her up a box of stuff after her mother booted her." Beth held out a hand toward the Singer, who supplied her with pen and paper. Beth started to scribble the address, then put the pen down.

"I only know if I go," she said. "I have terrible memory for directions and addresses. I have to see places. Landmarks. Then I can tell you which way to turn."

"This from the school brainiac?"

"It's in Sugar Land."

"That's too far away for her to be zoned to our school," I said. "That's even too far away for bussing."

"Then how'd she get in?"

"Probably the same way she does everything else." Magic. Manipulation. Whatever she needed to do to survive.

Mr. Landon wandered in from the back yard. He looked a little dazed around the edges. There were crickets in the rolled hems of his pants. "My grass is purple. Did you know that, Rude? What kind of spell did y'all do out there?"

The Singer met his gaze. Her words shimmered as they rolled off her tongue. "We'll fix it, Franklin. Why don't you hit the hay? We're fine here, especially now that Rude is up."

He yawned. "Wake me if you need something. Or when it's all over."

"Count on it."

He toddled a few steps, then paused as if he'd forgotten something. He started to glance over his shoulder.

The Singer sent more magic his way. "No worries, Franklin."

At that, he nodded before disappearing around the corner.

"It's going," the Singer said. "My gift."

"You're human."

"Not yet, but it's close. Just like with you and your demon."

My mouth curved in a wry smile. "I don't know whether to tell you I'm sorry."

"How about not?" She looked at Beth. "Thirty minutes to Melody's house?"

"Maybe more with the cars we'll have to move out of the way."

The Singer sighed. "If you have to see where we're going, we can't take my shortcut."

Under the ground. "Kevin told me about that. About how fast and asphyxiating it is. Also, if your faery powers go all the way—" I snapped my fingers "—then we'll be stuck under the ground. Any cars left here that we can borrow?"

"No," she said. "All gone."

"We can take the nearest abandoned one, then."

"Assuming the keys are in it."

Beth closed the book. "I can hotwire a car."

We looked at her.

"Theoretically, that is. I read how in a book."

We left a note for Mr. Landon in case the Singer's magic words wore off and he woke while we were gone. The dog refused to be left behind, so the four of us ventured out together.

The late morning sun stung my eyes badly enough that I went back inside and pilfered a pair of Kevin's sunglasses. They helped a little, but not completely. I still had a hard time looking at the expanse of the sky. Even the white wisps of the clouds dazzled too much.

A single crow perched in the ash tree that crowned the front yard. I met its beady gaze and thought hard at it.

Tell the others where we're going. Tell them to hurry.

The crow launched itself into the air, wheeling overhead twice before flying east.

Kevin and the others would have the information they needed. They would join us at Melody's place in time, or they'd be too late. I had no further control over that. I could only do what needed to be done.

I took a deep breath and focused on the soles of my feet, my connection to the ground. I felt my center of gravity in the bowl of my belly, conscious of the air playing on the edges of my skin. My magic crackled like cold lightning inside. The change was so close now, I could taste it.

"Rude?"

I looked at the Singer, at her very human features. "I'm all right for now."

Beth looked unconvinced. "Who the fuck is mowing the lawn in the middle of the apocalypse?"

I listened, picking up the unmistakable purr of a mower drifting from several blocks away. "Not sure I want to know."

"Are they a man or a monster?"

"The million dollar question. Let's go."

We walked in the direction of school past empty houses whose dark windows looked like hollow eyes. Cars crouched in some of the driveways, but most of them were locked behind garage doors. Made sense, seeing as the apocalypse had happened pretty late. A lot of people would've been home. We checked every one we could get to. None of them had keys inside—why would they?

Beth didn't like any of them for stealing, so we kept moving.

She watched her feet, following the uneven lines of asphalt patching the city used to fix the street. The Singer hummed to herself. I tried not to go crazy. Zach chased three squirrels. He caught zero.

The sign at the front of the school served as a reminder of what normal had been only a couple of days before.

Parent-Teacher Conferences – October 1

Homecoming – October 15

Go Cardinals!

Could we really get back there?

The lawn was littered with cigarette butts and crushed diet soda cans. One of the cheerleaders had left her pompoms propped against a brick pillar by the front door. The breeze rattled the red and white plastic, making the streamers look like tentacles.

In the front parking lot by the principal's office, we found an ancient four-door Chevy. No keys, but it had possibilities. Also, it smelled like week-old French fries, and ungraded homework covered the floorboards.

Beth sliced open the heel of her hand on the hard plastic of the steering column and she used some choice four-letter words that even

I wouldn't have, but she made the thing run. It had half a tank of gas. Good to go.

No one wanted me behind the wheel. No one wanted me as close to the wheel as the front seat, either. So Beth rode shotgun. The Singer drove.

It took her a while to get used to the fact that a four-door junker responded differently than a school bus. Too much lead foot on the gas pedal. Stopping short enough to leave rubber on the road and throw us into the rigid straps of our seat belts. I had to hold onto the dog to keep him from flying into the front of the car.

The Singer managed to get us to the freeway. Highway 69, headed south. She wove around an abandoned food truck to get us up the ramp and took it as easy as she could, finding us clear concrete to drive on. A billboards advertised the opening of the newest ice house —happy hour Monday through Friday from 2:00 to 4:00. The one after that, diamond rings guaranteed to make your girlfriend fall in love all over again. And the one after that, and the world's most badass exterminator service. Houston was a straight-up capitalist haven.

Beth squirmed in her seat. "What do you think will happen when we get there?"

"Besides my kicking Melody's ass?" the Singer asked.

"No offense, but she's getting more powerful and your juju's not exactly running on all cylinders."

"I'd almost forgotten how helpless I'm becoming, but now I feel so much better knowing that any minute I'm not going to be able to help my friends. Even better, I could become a liability."

"Sorry," Beth said.

The Singer shook her head. "No, I am. So you know, I did okay when I was human."

"Put the beat down on a lot of chicks, did you?"

That earned Beth a half-grin. "No. I only fought when I didn't have another option. But my right hook didn't suck."

I leaned forward and rested my forearms on the backs of their seats. "Everything Melody's done has been planned."

Beth shook her head. "She didn't plan to become evil."

"How can you possibly know that?"

"She's my friend, as much as she can be anyone's. She just wants to belong. She wants to be loved."

"And turning to her demon stepfather is the way to get that?"

"For someone who's supposed to have a lot of power, you're kind of dumb."

I narrowed my eyes.

She met my gaze via the rearview mirror. "Dude, do your parents love you?"

The question felt like a slap. Of course my parents loved me. "They—"

She interrupted. "They ignore you. And don't tell me it's because you're lucky, and they mostly refuse to acknowledge your existence because it fits with your need to sneak out in the middle of the night and never get grounded."

If her question had been a slap, that little speech felt like a clip of bullets emptied into my chest. "You don't know me."

"I'm observant."

"Observant?" She sounded like, I don't know, a librarian. No one else I knew used a word like that. I opened my mouth to say so, but the Singer glanced over her shoulder and the hard look on her face shut me down.

She knew what I felt, and what I was most likely to say. Hell, what anyone would say. For a self-righteous heartbeat, I wanted to tell them both where to go. Beth was off base and out of line. The Singer had no business looking at me like I was an asshole about to change the subject from the way my parents treated me to mock Beth's vocabulary because deflecting was easier than dealing.

A wave of rage rolled through me. I took a ragged breath and blew it out slowly. It barely helped. "You have no right to say all that to me."

Beth shrugged. "It's not about right. It's about humans."

The red-hot anger in me belonged to the demon inside, not the human. Didn't it? I couldn't tell, and that scared me as much or more than anything else that had happened since Melody found me at the pub, before she turned the world upside down.

"What about humans?" I asked.

"Humans do stupid things. I should know. I'm, like, a continual example of what not to do. We need things, and when we don't get them, the need just gets stronger until we find a way to fill it."

I thought about what Kevin said about my trying to be everyone's friend, always being the life of the party. Was needing to be seen such a bad thing? Was needing to be liked wrong?

The Singer's expression softened. "No one starts out wanting to be evil."

I flashed her ample side-eye.

She held up a hand. "Okay, *almost* no one starts out wanting to be evil. Most people think they're doing the right thing, or they start rationalizing that the terrible thing they're doing is the right thing. That's not just human nature. The fae can be that way, too. Anyone can, when the need they feel becomes the only thing that matters."

Maybe I understood Melody after all—not one-hundred-percent, because I'd never been in her shoes. Being ignored was bad, but that didn't mean I knew what it was like to have the shit beaten out of me or to be betrayed by my own flesh and blood. But as much as I wanted to stop her, I wanted to understand her. Maybe that was why Malek was so worried that I'd fall under her influence.

Becoming a demon didn't just mean transforming into a different species. It meant allowing every part of me to show up—especially the parts I didn't want anyone else to see because I felt ashamed of them, because I hated them. It meant giving those parts equal time and space, and sometimes letting them take over.

I could see Malek's point. How dangerous I truly could be.

"Singer, after you became fae, were you the same person as before, or were you totally different?"

She showed me a wry grin. "I'm helping you, aren't I?"

She'd helped us before. She'd given up the rest of her humanity for Kevin. She'd always been clear about whose side she was on. "That's not what I'm asking, exactly."

"You want to know whether you bring all of who you are along with you, good and bad?"

I nodded.

"The answer is yes. But you should stop thinking about some parts of you as 'bad' and other parts as 'good.' You're just you. Besides, you never know when any given quality will come in handy."

I couldn't imagine being glad to have a quality I rightfully hated. I couldn't picture for myself, or for anyone else. "What's mine?"

As soon as I asked the question, my anxiety rose like the mercury in a thermometer. I wanted to know what she thought. I feared what she'd say.

She didn't hesitate. "Ruthlessness."

I didn't feel worse, hearing that. I felt confused. "Where do you get that?"

"You do what needs to be done."

"I follow Oscar's orders."

"You've endured his training, passed all his tests. You break rules. You fight rogue fae and angels and demons, and anyone else magical who threatens your people. Ruthlessness is your number one shame, but it's also a strength. Not your greatest, though."

Her words quenched a thirst I didn't realize I had. I didn't spend a lot of time wondering what other people thought about me, and most of the time I didn't want to know. Other people's opinions of me were not my business. But I valued hers. I trusted her.

"Don't leave me in suspense, Singer."

"Your biggest strength is that you understand people. You imagine yourself in their place, what they're thinking, what they're feeling. You care about them, Rude. Your greatest challenge is that you care too much. You should watch yourself. I know what's happening in that heart of yours, and I don't like it."

How could she know when I didn't? Because she was fae, and this was about feelings. And suddenly I didn't want to hear another word about my strengths and weaknesses. "You sound like Malek."

"Malek doesn't trust you like I do."

I closed my eyes. To have my trust in her reciprocated, to know what she thought of me—

Too many feelings warred for control inside my heart. Too many contradictory thoughts. I felt cold, too, as if all the warmth had been drawn out of my body, leaving only ice.

I changed the subject. "Once Melody gets to her mom's house, she'll have the final ingredient of the spell, the one we didn't understand."

Beth bit her lip. "The blood of the guilty."

The Singer nodded. "Her mother. Her stepfather."

Beth laid a hand on the Singer's arm. With every word, her fingers tightened. "But she's not going to kill them, right? She just has to take their blood, like she has to take her own. That's all, right?"

I took in the color of Beth's light, which had gone from bright to sickly yellow. The library smell of her, gone from the comforting smell of old books to moldering paper. The confusion in her eyes. The prayer for reassurance in her grasp.

She wanted to believe that Melody was still the same girl she'd met at school. That no matter what else happened, Melody still had a moral center. Something innately human about her that made sense.

"No," I said.

Beth turned around in her seat to look at me.

"Watch the road," the Singer said.

"But—"

I sighed. "What her stepfather did to her—what her mother did— was unforgiveable. Do you really think she'll show them mercy? They didn't have any for her."

Beth's eyes filled with tears.

"Are you upset about what they did to her, or about what she'll do to them?" I asked.

"Yes," she said.

"I know a lot about gates between worlds. About what it takes to open them. If the spell calls for blood, no matter how powerful the blood, a little bit won't be enough. It'll have to be a lot. A sacrifice."

"She's going to sacrifice herself?"

I shook my head. "The spell revolves around her. She'll take just enough blood from herself to get the job done. She'll take the rest from the others. She'll sacrifice them."

"We have to stop her. We have to." She pounded the wheel with her fist.

"I know how you feel."

She glanced at me through the rearview mirror again. Her eyes accused me of lying for a moment, then gentled. "You want to save her."

The feeling was bigger than a want, more like a compulsion. "I need to."

"What if you can't, Rude?"

Then I would die trying. I didn't say that. I didn't even think it too loudly, out of fear that the Singer would hone in on how I felt.

It wasn't that I loved Melody. I barely knew her. And maybe the Singer was right that how much I cared about other people was a weakness, but it was part of who I was—and the part I was most afraid would disappear when the change finally took me.

"Rude," the Singer said. "Look behind us."

CHAPTER 12

I TURNED TO SEE a familiar police cruiser in our wake. I'd never felt so glad to see something familiar, even if it was the fae cops. Beth slowed until they caught us and pulled up alongside to our left. She lowered the windows and let in the stifling heat. They did the same.

Burns was behind the wheel of the cruiser. A sheen of sweat plastered his hair to his skull. Mud splotched his shoulder. "We were almost to Kevin's place when we got your message. How'd Melody escape?"

"Tell you when we get there," I said.

"Lead the way. We'll follow."

The Singer frowned, an edge of panic in her voice. "Wait."

"What is it?"

"Kevin's in trouble. Something very bad is about to happen."

I didn't see a single crow anywhere near us. I didn't hear any bird-like voices, and no images popped into my head. There was no new information coming at us. "How do you know that?"

"I feel him," she said. "The last of my fae-ness, connecting with his."

A breeze blew through the open windows, fluttering the feathers of her peacock halter and lifting her hair from her shoulders. She reached back for my hand, and I gave it to her without hesitation. Her grip was strong, and she turned to meet my gaze without blinking. Depths of time echoed in her eyes—the last of her fae immortality?

She brought all of herself to this moment. Everything she'd ever been and was now and ever would be. It humbled me. I understood in that instant why Kevin loved her.

"We need to go to him," she said. "Can you still vision?"

I thought I could, that there was still enough humanity and faery seer left in me. But if I did it, I might turn completely right here, right now. There might be nothing left of me, and then what would happen when it came to Melody and the demon she'd summoned?

I was supposed to put the big picture first. The city. All the people in it. I was supposed to play the long game, staying a step ahead of threats from the other realms. That was the job I trained for, my sworn duty. Anything else was stupid and foolish and a betrayal.

The long game was bullshit if it meant losing Kevin.

"Rude!"

I nodded. "Follow me."

"Get me close—as close as you can."

I closed my eyes again, bracing my body before forgetting about flesh and blood and bone. Kevin's face rose in my mind's eye. I focused on every feature: brown eyes, strong chin, the blade of his nose. I concentrated until every detail was solid. Until I could sense the sound of his voice. Until I smelled the place where he and Amy had gone to gather the water, green and murky.

A slender thread of intuition reached up from my center, winding its way up and around my spine. I grabbed hold of it as tightly as I dared, willing it not to break, willing it to take me where I needed to go.

My awareness shot through the roof of the car and into the cloudless, searing sky, rocketing over miles of road and concrete and steel. It slowed suddenly, dizzying on a downdraft, gentling into the branches of a water oak at the top of a grassy slope. The slope rolled toward the bayou. It looked wrong. The colors that should've been bright, muted. The mosquitos and gnats that danced above it, enticing my hunting instinct. The sunlight that speared the water like life-giving magic.

We have you.

The voice echoed in my consciousness. It wasn't mine. It wasn't the Singer's or Kevin's. It belonged to the crows in the oak's wind-brushed branches. I saw through their eyes, heard what they heard. Their senses were mine.

The muddy, green bayou smelled like wild water—rain, and water that'd seeped from the soil. The catfish that hugged the bottom. The snakes that slithered close to shore, and the people oblivious to all of that. The ones who'd come to gather the water that flowed into the city's heart. They stood among the reeds at the water's edge.

One human—Scott. Three who were not—Malek, the god with his poisoned blood, and Kev, almost completely fae now, his wingspan astonishing. Emotions flowed off of him like lava from an erupting volcano.

And Amy, who stood knee-deep in the water, tilted forward because of the steep angle of the earth beneath the surface. Who the crows marked among the not-human. I didn't understand.

The sun glinted off the current—and off of Malek's bald head. Scott said something that made Amy laugh, a brittle laugh that the slightest touch could shatter into a million shards. The wind blew her hair into a tangle of blue-black feathers. She unscrewed the top to the mason jar and handed the lid to Malek.

I felt the Singer's presence, the shine of her consciousness beside me. The scent of patchouli. She focused on Amy, and then beyond Amy, deeper into the bayou. Where the current rippled strangely, as if something else was in the water. Something that shouldn't be there.

It raced toward Amy with lightning speed.

Kev saw it first. He shouted a warning and reached for Amy. His fingers caught only the hem of her T-shirt as the thing in the bayou punched up, the water exploding into spray. Its fist struck Amy's midsection.

The blow stole her breath. She fell forward, hitting the water flat.

The thing grabbed her hair with one green hand and dragged her and the empty jar under the surface.

Kev dove in after her. A second presence shot from the opposite shore, raising a wave in its wake.

The crows launched from the branches, cawing and wheeling, shadows feathering the bayou's surface. My sight broke into fragments, bits and pieces overlapping in confusion.

Scott, running into the water. Malek, stopping him with an outstretched arm and holding him on the shore by force.

The second creature colliding with Kevin underwater, forcing him down, dragging him to the bottom. Darkness swallowed them. I couldn't see them. I couldn't feel them.

I couldn't reach Kevin like this. I couldn't do a damn thing.

The Singer shouted. The crows cried. Their voices sounded like hers. They spoke one word.

"Kevin!"

The sound was magic, pure and true and filled with the last of the Singer's fae power. It rang over the water and into the deep. Light flashed in the murk. Kevin's light.

Then the Singer's presence vanished, leaving me alone inside the vision.

The birds turned again. I saw only Amy. She tangled with the first creature, swimming beneath the water as if she was born to it, magic flowing off of her in copper waves. Air bubbles popped on the surface, the fight close and deadly underneath.

Dark red blood fogged the bayou and the thrashing ceased. Amy's head broke the surface. She was covered in blood. None if it looked to be hers.

Then she dove, moving faster than her attacker had, bolting toward the bottom. Toward Kevin.

I held my breath, heart hammering, the rush of my own blood drowning the caws of the crows and Scott's curses and Malek's silence.

The surface rippled. An eternal moment later, two rose to the surface. Amy put Kevin in a lifeguard hold and swam him to shore, pushing him up and out of the water, where Scott and Malek could grab his arms and haul him onto the grass. He sank to his knees, coughing up water, shaking water off his wings like a wet dog.

Amy didn't follow.

She went under again, coming up this time not entirely free of blood, but cleaner, facing away from the group. The ripple of muscles in her back startled me—and worse, as soon as my eyes processed that not only had she seemingly lost her shirt and bra, I wasn't looking at muscle under the skin. I was looking at gills.

"Holy Jesus," Scott said.

Kevin followed his gaze. "Oh, my god."

"It's fine," Amy said. But she didn't so much as glance over her shoulder at him.

"You have magic now," he said. "You killed that thing—whatever it was—in the water."

"It's what I wanted." She took a deep breath and blew it out slowly, diving again, this time for the center of the bayou, for the current at its heart.

Kev pushed to his feet, lurching into Malek and grabbing him by the shirt collar. "What did you do to her?"

Malek pushed him back. *I gave her peace.*

"How is this peace?"

The water's safe for her. It can take her emotions. Defuse the ticking bomb.

"What bomb? What are you talking about?"

She's hurting, Kevin. She wasn't built for the world you live in. She wanted to be there because of you. If she hadn't come to me, she'd have done something drastic.

"Like diving into the bayou and turning into a…a mermaid?"

She's—was—suicidal.

"I would've seen it. I would know."

She wouldn't let you.

"You're full of shit."

Think what you want.

Think.

I thought back to the vision where I'd seen Malek and Amy together. How there were parts of the conversation I didn't grok. How, hearing him talk to Kevin, I finally did.

Kev didn't want to believe it—I read that in the way his mouth pulled wide, the sudden anguish in his eyes, the catch of his breath. But Malek wasn't stupid, and he wasn't, contrary to popular belief, evil. He gave humans what they craved most and it was up to them to manage the consequences. If he didn't like you, watch out.

He liked Amy. My animal instinct, magnified by the birds', told me it was more than that. He understood Amy. He felt protective of her. Surely, Kev had to see that.

Kevin leaned forward, resting his hands on his thighs, his voice a whisper. "Why didn't she say something?"

She was protecting you.

"I never asked for that."

It doesn't matter. She's not going to be able to stay with you. She needs the peace of the water, at least for now. She can bring you what you need, but she stays behind when you leave.

"No."

It's not up to you.

Kevin's face contorted in anger. "You did this."

No, Kevin. She did. She'll be all right.

Kevin shook his head.

It'll be all right.

"No," Kevin said. "It won't."

Amy scissor-kicked and turned, bringing the water back to shore. She came close enough that the swell of her breasts showed above the water. Close enough to see that the anxiety had washed from her face. She was serene. No other way to describe it.

She handed the jar off to Malek, who held his ground. He wouldn't move for Kevin to slip past. He handed the jar and the lid to Scott and signed to Kev.

You want to talk to her, do it from there.

"I want it to be private."

Not right now.

Because Kevin would try to talk her out of what she'd done. And when he couldn't do that, he'd try to pull her out by force. He may not be a water fae, like Amy had become, but he carried fae power. His magic was not inconsiderable, and he had more experience using it than she did.

Kev wiped his eyes. "Amy, why?"

"I need this, Kevin. I can't live without it—at least, not right now. I did the best I could. I didn't leave you in the lurch. I got what you needed. You can make the water now. You can save the city. Put everything back to normal."

"Everything except you."

She sighed. "Kevin, I'm not a thing you can fix."

Kevin knelt shakily in the tall reeds. "I didn't want to hurt you."

She started to speak twice before finding the right words. "This isn't about you."

"But I made it worse."

"This is about me. Who I am. What I need. And you couldn't have changed a thing. You can't change who you are, and neither can I. I was like this before."

"If you'd told me, I would've listened."

"Thanks." She seemed to mean that.

In the end, it didn't matter. She'd gone to Malek. He'd given her what she wanted most, and that was that.

"You should go now, Kevin," she said.

He held her gaze. "I can't leave you."

"You have to. You and Scott."

Malek snapped his fingers.

Kevin met his gaze.

I'll stay. I'll watch over her. I promise I won't leave her.

We needed Malek to meet us at Melody's, to help us handle her and the demon. He couldn't stay here.

He heard my thoughts, broadcast loud and clear through the crows. He glanced up at the birds and shook his head. He was with Amy.

Whether we lived or died was up to us.

Kevin heard the exchange. He understood what had happened, what was going on. He refused to move. It took Scott sliding his hands under Kevin's arms and physically turning him around.

Scott glanced at the birds as Malek had. "I hope you're watching, Rude. If there's anything else you need us to know, spit it out now. He's the one who can hear you and he's about to lose his shit. You've got, like, ten seconds."

I spoke Melody's address. Kevin repeated it to Scott.

Scott put him in the Explorer and left rubber on the asphalt as he peeled out of the parking lot. I heard Kevin's screams through the glass before I pulled myself out of there.

I slammed back into my body, inside the Chevy, my hand in the Singer's. Her skin felt hot, and mine like ice. My heart felt full of hurt, full to the brim with pain. I ached until the feeling leached from every inch of my body and every drop of my soul.

I opened my eyes. The Singer had opened hers, too. She held my gaze long enough for me to see the last of the fae spark leave them. And with the departure of the spark, her wings dissolved into shadows.

Shock shook me. I let go of her hands.

A single tear slid down her cheek.

Beth's eyes widened, her mouth falling open.

I struggled to make sense of what I felt. Of words that wanted to come out of my mouth. The Singer was fully human. Amy was a mermaid. Kevin was wild with grief and now whatever fae connection he'd felt with the Singer was gone.

The flat sound of my voice scared me. "Kevin and Scott are on their way."

Stacy bolted out of the cruiser, making a beeline for the front passenger door of the Chevy. She yanked it open and gathered the Singer, pulling her from the vehicle and holding her up when she couldn't stand. "You need to come with us. You and Beth."

"Why?"

"Because Rude looks like he's going off the deep end, and you can't be in the car with him when that happens."

I didn't feel like I was losing it. I felt fine. Relaxed, as if everything would be all right now, as if the world was somehow right. I couldn't even remember why I'd been so freaked out about it before.

I felt the way Amy the mermaid had looked.

Beth exited the car in a hurry. Zach went with her, the first time he'd been willing to leave my side. He glanced back at me twice, whining, the hairs along his spine rising as if I were the enemy. It shattered my heart into a million pieces, each one ripping a hole in my chest.

I didn't understand any of it. I hadn't done anything wrong.

Stacy snapped her fingers to get my attention. "If you're going to Melody's, you have to drive yourself. If we get there and you're in league with her, we'll take you down or we'll take you out."

My rage grew with every word she'd spoken. I growled a response. "There's nothing wrong with me."

She acted as if I hadn't said anything. "Do you understand?"

I slid out of the back seat, slamming the door harder than I intended, and climbed behind the wheel, glaring at them all. It hit me like a fall of bricks that none of them had the power to stop me from doing whatever I wanted. The freedom of that rushed through my blood like a drug.

"Good luck, Rude."

I focused on the Singer, still in Stacy's arms and halfway to the cruiser. She'd forced the witch to stop so that she could look at me. There was nothing magical about her anymore. She was just an ordinary girl with an extraordinary voice and all the wisdom of human and fae in her sharp eyes. She showed none of the fear or anger that Stacy did. She gazed at me as if I were still the Rude Davies she knew, responsible and dependable and strong.

"We'll be right behind you," she said.

She trusted me in spite of my transformation. I felt it like an arrow to the heart.

What would the faery seer apprentice I'd been do now? I couldn't begin to guess. I only knew I needed to get to Melody before her father arrived in the human world. I didn't know whether I could save her, or whether she wanted to be saved, only that I had to try.

I put the pedal to the metal, praying that I'd get there in time, and that the others would arrive in time to back me up. As I left rubber on the road, images and sounds sent by the crows watching Melody's house flooded my mind.

Pleas for mercy, unanswered. The thunk of a blade into flesh and bone. The spill of blood.

Melody had begun the summoning.

I didn't have to be magically connected to her to feel what she felt. The inescapable draw of the demon inside. The way it overtook who she had been and obliterated who she wished she could be.

In the end, she'd do anything to bring her father here, to keep him on this plane. Anything to belong.

Anything to be loved.

CHAPTER 13

I ZOOMED IN TO Melody's driveway as the sun sank into the horizon, washing the sky in orange, indigo, and gold. The fat moon hung high and full as if it were midnight. My watch read 12:00.

Time was confused. Reality was confused. A demon powerful enough to destroy the world hovered just on the other side of a portal to our world. How could we fight something that strong? How could I?

While I'd been with the others, I could hide behind who I'd always been with them. The go-to guy. The good guy. The one who always knew what to do. Without them, I had only the demon in me, shredding my insides bloody as it clawed its way to the surface. So little of the good guy remained, I feared he wouldn't matter.

I wished I had Zach with me. It would've been good to have him at my side. It would've helped me not to be so afraid of what I might do. But that was just it: I couldn't lean on anyone else, not anymore. No one else could choose for me. This moment belonged to me. I would stand or I would fall, and the world would follow.

Stepping out of the car took monumental courage. Taking the first step and putting one foot in front of the other after that felt even harder.

The house of Melody's nightmares looked like any other from the outside. Cookie-cutter one-story brick job with big, blind picture windows on either side of the entrance gate. A young pine had been planted on either side of the pebbled front walk. I could smell not only the green of their needles, but the resin inside their bark, and beneath all of that, the fertilizer that had been applied to the grass before the big magical bang. The chemical smell made me feel instantly nauseated.

The crows in the trees squawked at me. They were carrion birds, like crows and ravens. When they weren't singing for their supper in grocery store parking lots, they picked apart dead things with beaks and claws and took flight, carrying souls to the afterlife. I knew how they felt.

I expected to be struck by lightning in that moment. Or for Melody to come outside and throw everything bit of magic she had at me. But nothing stopped me from turning the knob on the unlocked door.

The stench struck me first. Blood. Guts. Burnt offering.

My sneakers squeaked on the tile floor as I followed my nose. Past the half bath and around the small atrium where Melody's mom had planted lemon trees and ivy. Into the living room, where heavy antique furniture sat sentry and dust motes floated in the air. Down the hall where the walls were lined with family photos filled with smiling people with fearful eyes. The hall led past the master bedroom to the smaller one that once had belonged to Melody.

My feet sank into the plush blue carpet as soon as I stepped inside. The bed had been broken down, the frame turned wheels-up and stacked in pieces against the far wall, mattress upright beside it. The desk had been chopped into respectable firewood, the laptop that'd been on top of it thrown into a corner. Built-in bookshelves held a horde of teddy bears, from half-shredded to mint condition.

Melody had made a circle of her blood in the center of the space— I knew it was hers because of the scent and the color and the light, even though she'd burned it until it blackened. Inside the circle, she'd laid out the body of her stepfather, his wrists and ankles tied to metal tent stakes she'd driven through the floor with the hammer that lay by his head.

He had salt-and-pepper hair and a groomed mustache and beard, manicured hands and a shiny wedding ring. He wore a red golf shirt and khakis, not a scuff on his white tennis shoes. He didn't look like a villain. He looked like Joe Suburbia, salary of at least one hundred thousand a year. Probably he volunteered for the homeowners association or the neighborhood watch and had a lot of friends.

This everyday human being was the monster who'd hurt Melody, and we were worried about her summoning a monster who might love her. Who was right here? Who was wrong?

For a heartbeat, I teetered on that tightrope. When had everything become so messed up? When had family and friends known that something was wrong with Melody? Had they said or done something, or pretended, or looked the other way because it wasn't their kid brutalized? Maybe they hadn't thought it was their problem.

The stepdad had a dozen wounds that gaped like open mouths. His blood stained the carpet so thickly and deeply, it'd never come out. Melody knelt in the blood between his feet. Her hair stuck out in all different directions as if she'd stuck all he fingers in electrical outlets. His blood soaked the front of her overalls and streaked the skin of her shoulders and arms. She'd wiped her face with the white washcloth clutched in her hands. The smear of red on the bright white shocked me.

She'd created this…this horror. She'd killed a man, and even if he'd deserved killing, what she'd done to him was beyond belief.

He moaned. Not dead, not yet. He could be saved. If I could just—

I shook my head to clear it. There was no way to help him even if I wanted to. No ambulance or life helicopter. There was only Melody, her demon father, and me.

"Hey." Melody kept her gaze locked on her dying enemy.

I stepped toward her.

"No closer, Rude."

"Or what?"

She took a shuddering breath. "I'll have to kill you, too. Don't make me do that."

Physically, I was bigger and stronger. That worked in my favor if we fought. But the power that rose in answer to her threat bore no trace of the seer's magic I knew. It tasted like forgetting—like the one and only night I'd drunk so much that I'd blacked out. Far from feeling terrified at the loss of control, I'd felt grateful for it because it meant I could be someone else. I could be anybody except myself.

I had no memory at all of what I'd done, but the way my friends had looked at me the next day—the way Oscar had looked at me—it'd been bad.

I understood, finally. The transformation Melody's magic had caused in me meant going back to that place. If I started down that road, I might never come back.

She glanced at me from the corner of her eye.

I held up my hands to signal a temporary truce and crouched on the blood-soaked carpet until we saw eye-to-eye.

"Blood of the guilty," I said.

She nodded. "I'm glad you came. I don't think I could stand being alone in this."

"Is that what you want from me? Company?"

She turned toward me. She looked exactly the same as she had on the night she'd blown up our world—small and scared. Then the fear vanished, and a smile graced her lips. "A smart guy like you should've figured it out by now."

She was drawn to me like I was drawn to her. It was more than an attraction between the demon in her and the demon in me. The feeling felt human, too.

I struggled with what to say. The wrong words could wound, and I didn't want to hurt her. Not like that.

"You're really going to leave me hanging, Rude?"

I shook my head. "We have this problem to deal with first."

"It's only a problem if you let it be."

"Disappearing of millions of people. Turning the rest into

monsters. Bringing a demon into the world that could destroy everything that remained."

"They deserve it. They let this happen to me."

I sucked in a breath.

"I'm not the only one," she said. "There are people who have it so much worse. And everyone pretends nothing's wrong. They just go on living their lives while we're hurt and killed, or thrown away like garbage. I'm doing this for all of us."

Whether or not I believed she was acting for her siblings in suffering, she did. "Destroying the world is better than letting it go on the way it has."

Her eyes filled with angry tears. "Damn right."

"Melody—"

"Will you help me or not?"

"I was always gonna help you, remember?"

"Finish the spell and bring my father here so you can kill him."

"That was the plan."

"You won't be able to do it, Rude. When he gets here, the demon inside you will obey him. Anything he asks, you'll do it gladly. If you really care about your friends, you wouldn't have come here. Now, they'll have to fight you, too."

She was right. Stacy was right. The singer was wrong. I'd screwed up everything by coming here. I started to stand. If I could get outside, I could use the crows to warn the others away. If they never showed with the spell ingredients, then they'd be safe. Wouldn't they?

What did that word even mean anymore?

Melody read my face. She knew my thoughts. "Sit."

My legs refused to obey me. They obeyed her. I fell to the bloody carpet, landing hard on my ass.

I opened my mouth to shout. If I could yell loudly enough, the crows would hear me through the window.

"Shut up," she said.

The hell was happening to me? When did I become a slave to her will? When the last of the faery seer's magic left me. That was when I'd lost my power over her. She'd had a while to finger out how her magic worked. She knew the ins and outs better than I did. She was in control here.

"Your friends are going to come here with the items we need. When they get here, we'll take those things from them and give them my father."

I narrowed my eyes. We were supposed to use those ingredients against him, to drive him away.

"Like I said before, Rude—for someone so smart, you should've figured it out by now."

The ingredients represented the heart of the land, the spirit of this place, this city. If Melody gave them to her father, he'd have dominion over them. He'd be tied to the land, not forced out. This place would become his home, his anchor in our world.

"Kind of brilliant, right? And after your friends make that possible, they'll have served their purpose. Then, they'll get what they deserve, too."

Brilliant? Yes, it was. She'd played us from the start. Played me. I wanted to believe she still had some good in her heart, that she could be saved, and she'd taken advantage. She was the smart one, and I was stupid, allowing my feelings to get in front of my brain.

That was what Malek had feared. I'd done everything he predicted I'd do, and worse. I'd set up my friends for a world of hurt.

I spat words, surprised when Melody didn't silence me. "What do you have against them? They tried to help you."

"Beth, maybe."

"Maybe? She took you in. She literally helped you decipher the spell you cast on all of us."

"She feels sorry for me. That's not something a real friend does. I don't need anyone's pity."

Of course not. She needed love. That was why she'd summoned her father in the first place. But did she know what love was?

"Why do you care so much about those people, Rude? Why does it matter to you so much what happens to them?"

It was more than them. I cared about everyone Melody's spell had hurt. I cared about every person I met.

But my friends were in a different class. The singer, who trusted me in spite of myself. Stacy, who wasn't afraid to call me on my shit. Scott, dependable even though he had no magic and the situations we dragged him into were much more dangerous for him than the rest of us. Amy, who did the right thing no matter how much her heart hurt. And Kevin, who was brave as fuck and had my back no matter what.

"They're family," I said.

"Family is your parents, Rude."

"They are, yeah. Family by blood. I love them."

"Whether they deserve it or not."

"All this talk about what people deserve—what if we all deserve good and bad? We're both. We do the right thing. We screw up. We hurt people."

She shook her head.

"You don't think what you do matters?"

"All that matters is what they did to me, Rude. And your friends are just the same. They saw what was happening. They didn't do anything."

"What could they possibly have done? We aren't kids, but adults don't listen to us. We didn't have the power to help you."

She stared at me. For a moment, I thought I'd gotten through to her, but then her expression closed. She not only hadn't heard a word I'd said, she didn't want to.

"Who made you judge, jury, and executioner?" she asked.

I could ask her the same question. I didn't, though. What was the point?

The circle she'd laid in the floor began to smoke, carpet fibers glowing like coals before catching, flames rising in spirals.

Melody's breath caught in her throat.

THE SPOT WHERE HER stepfather lay began to blacken. The man shuddered, breathing in once more before his chest fell a final time, slowly and painfully. The darkness beneath him opened up like a sinkhole, swallowing the top half of his body as Melody scrambled back. She barely cleared the body before the hole grew large enough to take it all.

"Yes!" she whispered.

A rush of blistering cold rose from the black, slicking Melody's cheeks with ice and frosting her lashes. Her breath fogged the air, then froze in crystalline form, falling like hail. She turned all of her attention toward the opening.

I pushed to my feet, preparing to flee or fight as blue sparks began to float from the darkness. They should've been hot, but they radiated the kind of cold that could freeze a human being solid before they could call out. But not me. To me, the cold felt like home—the home I'd never known, where I could be recognized. Where I could be known completely. No more living with people who acted as if I didn't exist. No more hiding how much that hurt.

Even the possibility of that enchanted me, casting its own spell and wrapping me in chains of desire that I didn't want to break. So, I didn't run. I didn't call out. I stood there, mesmerized for a long moment. I wanted it to last forever, to always be a promise.

Melody's father began to rise through the hole in the floor. He didn't look like a demon—I could see through him, as if he was a ghost. He'd been summoned, but he hadn't yet fully arrived. He couldn't until Kevin and the others brought the rest of the magical elements to the scene.

The demon wore a human face. Thick black hair flowed in waves to his linebacker's shoulders, skin the color of frost, and eyes like mine—no whites, only black pupils. He wore jeans and a powder-blue button-down with the sleeves rolled to the elbows, feet stuffed into broken-in brown boots. He beamed at Melody the way I'd always wanted my father to smile at me, as if he was proud of what she'd become. A halo of magic the color of blood radiated from him, its edges undulating in the breeze generated by his power like snakes, fangs bared and throats hissing.

Melody searched his face, her expression equal parts hope and anticipation and fear. She reached for my hand, fingers trembling. Waves of desperation flow from her, tangled with her magic, turning her power into a chaotic mess.

She was still very powerful, very dangerous. It was my goddamn job to defeat her. To do everything I could—to give my life if necessary—to stop what she'd started, to reverse the spell. To save us all.

Melody didn't look like a monster. I saw through her the way I saw through her father. She was just a girl about to meet her father for the first time. Maybe he was the answer to her prayers. Maybe he would love her.

I needed to be close, whatever he chose.

I closed the distance between us in two long strides, twining my fingers with hers. Her skin felt as icy as mine did. I could hear her heartbeat as if it were in my chest. The same adrenaline that coursed through her veins ran in mine.

Her father's voice broke the sensation, sending lightning through my nerves, making my stomach feel weightless and heavy at the same time, as if it were tumbling head-over-heels through space.

"Is this the offering you've brought me?"

Not *Hey, it's been a lifetime,* or *I'm so glad to see you,* or even *Thank you for bringing me here.* He didn't care about her at all. His pride was about what she'd done for him, not who she was.

He didn't acknowledge for even a second the man Melody had killed and let fall into the opening. He wasn't talking about her stepdad as an offering. He didn't mean me, either. He meant Melody.

She furrowed her brow. "The spell said—"

"The spell calls for the wild earth, the wild water, and the blood of the one who summoned me."

She shook her head. "That's not how this works. It's the blood of the guilty."

"You did this," I whispered. "You summoned him. You broke the world. You killed."

She squeezed my hand so tightly, the small bones ground together. "Shut up."

Her father barreled on as if neither of us had spoken. "Thank you for making this easy for me."

She tried again. "You're my father."

The demon stared at her.

"But you can't hurt me."

Her words had no visible effect. He continued to stare. With each passing second, I felt more like an ant beneath a magnifying glass on a sunny day.

There was no appealing to the demon's sense of family. He didn't have one. Even partially here in our world, half-solid, half as powerful as he would be when he fully arrived, he could still hurt her. He could still kill.

I tightened my grip on her as she'd done to me. "Melody."

She yanked her hand from mine with so much force, she lost her balance. She backpedaled, tripping over her feet, and started to go over.

I reached for her, fingertips brushing her arm as she fell.

Her father moved toward her—not to help. He eyed her like a predator about to strike.

I stepped between them.

He flicked his finger at me as if swatting away a fly. It hit me like a punch from a heavyweight Olympic boxer times ten. My head rocked back and my feet left the floor. My vision blackened, consciousness fleeting—until I slammed into something hard and dropped like a stone, face-first to the floor.

I grabbed on to shreds of awareness, blinking until I could see colors and shapes. Until I recognized the nubby substance under my hands as carpet. Until I made out Melody and the demon across the room.

She was on her back, on the floor. He loomed over her, hands balled into fists. His lips moved, but I couldn't hear what he said. I could only feel the gathering storm of magic as he spoke.

I tasted his intent and read it in the icy threads of light and darkness that snaked around him. The spell he intoned would kill her.

I tried to call up my power, the seer's magic that had helped me in countless fights, that had saved my life and Kevin's and so many others'. It didn't answer. There was nothing left of it. Not even a drop to scrape from the bottom of the well. All I had was the magic of my worst nightmare. Of my own demon.

That power was rage. That power was a demand to be seen. *I won't be ignored. I won't be shunned.* It rose in me until it rippled beyond the edges of my skin.

I didn't understand it. I didn't know what it would do when I unleashed it. But it was all I had.

I let it fly.

A cloud of dark gray mist rippled through the air, latching on to the demon, clinging to his not-quite-there form. For a heartbeat, I held my breath, waiting for it to hurt him.

Then the mist sank into him, my magic invading his. Any second now, he would feel it. He'd fight or retreat.

He did none of those things.

He absorbed the power I'd thrown at him. It wove with his magic as if it belonged to him. He absorbed it, and it made him stronger.

I heard a strangled cry, startled when I realized it'd come from my own mouth.

Magic rose in me again. I raged with it, spearing the demon with everything I had. I only made him more powerful.

I pushed to my knees, rocked back on my heels, and screamed my throat raw. I was the same as Melody's father, only weaker. I was nothing here. I meant nothing. I was everything my family believed me to be.

I poured out my anger, all my anguish. There was so much, it would never run dry.

Melody's voice broke through the wrenching sound. She spoke a single word. My name.

CHAPTER 15

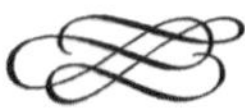

I INHALED A RAGGED BREATH and met her gaze as the demon knelt beside her, pinning her against the blood-soaked carpet with the flat of a wiry hand. I glimpsed a glint of silver from the corner of my eye—the blade she'd used to slice up her stepfather, just out of her reach. She stretched for it, the tips of her fingers brushing the hilt. She couldn't grasp it. She needed it.

She needed me.

Even if I couldn't overpower her father. Even if couldn't win. Even if the fight killed me.

It didn't matter who she was or what she'd done. It only mattered that she was in my care, because I was the only one here who could help her. A few days ago, I'd been a faery seer's apprentice. Now, I was the only faery seer in town.

No matter that my training was incomplete. No matter that the fae magic had abandoned me. She was my responsibility.

That was what I'd promised Oscar. More, it was what I promised the city, the land, and the spirits of this place on the night I'd taken my first oaths in the park downtown where the willow once stood.

I might be a demon now because of Melody's spell, but I carried all of who I was to this moment. I couldn't choose what I felt, but I could choose to act.

I chose to honor my heart. I chose to honor my oaths.

Muscles shaking, I scrambled to my feet. I lurched toward them, legs barely holding me.

The demon glanced at me. Just a split second.

In the space of a breath, Melody stretched her hand and her will toward the blade, fingers wrapping around the end of the hilt, dragging it into her grip. She slashed fast and hard.

Not her father, who wanted and needed her dead. She sliced her free arm, wrist to elbow, spilling her bright blood.

The hell was she doing?

Making the sacrifice—the blood of the guilty.

Had she done it to bring her father fully into this world so that we could kill him? Or to gift him dominion over us all and a home in the human realm?

A boom rang out from the front of the house—the door slammed open. Footfalls on the tile. Headed toward us.

I wheeled, ready to defend or attack, as Kevin ran into the room, wings folded tightly against his back. The jar of living water, lid on tight, sloshed in his hands.

He raked me with his gaze, eyes widening. His magic flared deep green, like a forest after a storm. As if he expected me to strike him.

I stepped back, moving out of the way as the others piled in behind him. Scott, hands curled into fists. Stacy, carrying the jar of living flame. The Singer, striding into the room wholly human. Even without a drop of magic in her, she shone like a star.

She opened her mouth and began to sing, gifting the demon her breath—more than that, with her story. She mesmerized us. All of us, including the demon.

She sang of a man who wore suits everywhere he went. Of the childhood he prepared for her. Strolls through the park. Finger paintings. Her first chemistry set. The puppy that grew into a strong dog who became her best and only friend until he turned gray around his whiskers and died of old age. She fell in love. She discovered her own voice.

She sang every night at the club. Musicians joined with her. They became a band. One night a mysterious stranger sat in the front row. He kissed her hand after the set and, after that, she began to grow wings.

She lost everything that ever made her human except one. Love. Even when she couldn't feel it close—even when it felt so far away she thought she might never feel anything again—she kept her faith in it.

Her song became pure then. Ecstasy. Sex. Raw life force that couldn't be denied. The seed that grew and pushed up through the earth to reach for the sun. The molten fire beneath the earth that burst forth and created new land. The hand of God that touched each newborn thing and gifted a spark of soul.

She never lost her faith in life. In love.

In Kevin.

Who opened the jar of water Amy had filled and spoke a word of power over it so that the liquid glowed with intelligence and magic. He drew back his arm and threw it full force at the demon. The glass shattered against the demon's chest, drenching him in living water.

The demon's edges became defined. Solid. Real.

Stacy handed the jar of living flame to Kevin. He threw it, too. The glass broke as it struck the demon's chest, flames singeing where they licked his skin.

The demon's breath fogged the air.

Scott reached into his pocket and pulled out a bulb of red cloth tied at the neck with string. The living earth.

He handed the bulb to Kevin, who woke it with another word of magic. He met my gaze, a question in his eyes.

The earth was the final element of life, the one that would bring the demon fully here. The one that would either give him what Melody had promised or be turned against him. Could I do what needed to be done? Did I even know what that was?

I held out my hand. Kevin tossed me the earth. The scent that escaped the cloth as it landed in my palm was the perfume of the thick, packed brown and gray clay soil that I loved. How could I give that to the demon?

Maybe it wasn't about giving anything to the demon. Maybe it was about the love I felt for the city and the land, and the oaths I'd taken. It went beyond Melody or Kevin or Stacy—beyond any individual human or fae I cared about and felt responsible for. It went to the heart of this place, and the connection we'd forged.

All my training had prepared me to fight and die for the city. For the world. But connection was a two-way street, and if I was going to keep the promises I'd made, then I prayed that the land would need to keep its promise to me.

I strode toward the demon, the gift of living earth in my hand, knowing in my heart that it would never be a weapon. It existed. It lived and breathed and protected and provided for all who lived on and within it. It was a fact. It was the truth.

The demon's lips curved in anticipation. It waited to be given its due.

As I closed the distance between us, I kept my eyes on him—his writhing magic, his entitled, arrogant face, and his eyes, which had shaded from black to blue, like his daughter's. I tried not to see the blood that poured from her arm or how it darkened the carpet, how pale her skin had become, how her eyes closed as her consciousness fled.

My voice sounded as if it belonged to someone much stronger than I felt. "Do you want this?"

The demon reached out a hand.

I placed the earth in his grasp. I covered his hand with mine, and I pulled him to me with every ounce of strength and will I possessed. I wrapped my arms around him, heedless of the still-burning flames on his skin, and whispered.

"Take it, if you can."

His magic sliced into me like an arrow, straight and true, aimed for my heart. It wasn't enough to draw to himself the thing I'd offered. He had to grab for more than that. He had to take my life.

I closed my eyes. I put all my faith in the one power that could save me—save us all.

The demon froze. His body began to tremble. He dropped the bulb of earth into the pool of his daughter's blood.

I drew back just enough to look him in the eye. His eyes widened in surprise.

The magic I'd thrown at him—the rage and anguish that had no effect on him, that had only seemed to make him stronger—darkened beneath his skin, blackening his veins, tearing apart the blood vessels and the cells, destroying him from the inside out.

He pushed away, staggering toward the hole he'd risen from. "How?"

"Your greed," I said. "Your violence."

"But you're not even a shadow compared to me. You're—"

"Nothing?"

He stared at me, mouth open.

The power of earth surged beneath my feet, flowing like lava from the bedrock through the foundation of the house, through the floor, climbing into my legs and filling me full to overflowing. The flames that had licked the demon's skin now danced across mine. The water that had drenched him slid along my body, soaking my clothes and quenching my thirst. I breathed in the stench of copper, the blood that Melody had shed, and I forgave her. The echoes of the Singer's story filled my ears and tumbled into my memory.

"The land has my back," I said. "The city defends me."

"I'm more powerful than your city," he said. But he backed toward the lip of the whole from which he'd risen.

"Not today."

He fell into the darkness.

The room flashed black and then white before my eyes, then my vision cleared and my legs gave way. I fell to my knees in Melody's blood. The others moved around us, kneeling beside her, binding her wound.

There was only so much they could do for her.

The demon had fled, but he wasn't dead.

The world remained a nightmare.

CHAPTER 16

KEVIN STOOD WITH his winged back against the Explorer's passenger door, his face buried in the Singer's shoulder while she held him, her wings tucked neatly out of the way. Scott and Stacy sat in the grass, holding hands, shell-shocked.

Melody lay in the grass before them, her chest barely rising and falling, color leached from her skin. Beth cradled Melody's head in her lap, smoothing her hair over and over again, like a benediction.

Melody wouldn't get any better than that until we found a way to fix the hellhole around us, but she wouldn't get any worse, either. Fae magic and witchery had seen to that.

I wanted her to be all right. More than that, I needed her to be.

I met Stacy's gaze and read the same emotion. She would help Melody if she could. It would have to be enough.

Reid's harsh voice broke the stillness. "What now, Rude?"

I glanced at him and his partner. They stood in the middle of the street in front of their cruiser, Zach barking in the front seat, nose tilted toward the cracked passenger window. They hadn't entered the house at all. They'd been the rear guard, in case we failed and the demon had made it out. Now, they were at loose ends, just like the rest of us.

The nightmare Melody had conjured was still with us. The question was, what were we going to do about it?

What was I going to do about it?

A murder of crows perched in the trees, their chilly eyes fixed on me. The air smelled like ozone, fried and filled with static electricity and the copper stain of blood. I didn't think I'd ever smell anything else again.

I cleared my throat. "We need to go."

The Singer pulled away from Kevin. "Yes, we need to go. You have your own work to do, seer. But Kevin and I have got to go to Faery. There's trouble there that whatever you're about to do won't fix. It's up to us."

I stared at them. "I don't understand."

"Yes, you do," Kev said. "I trust you, Rude. You got this."

I had only one card left to play. "I hope to hell you're right."

"We'll be back as soon as we can, man."

I laid a hand on his arm, and he looked at me with fae eyes. I tried to see my friend in them. He was in there, somewhere. "What do you want me to tell your dad?"

"The truth."

I nodded.

"Take care of Amy?"

"That's a promise."

He reached around and hugged me fiercely, then followed the Singer over to where Burns and Reid waited.

The four of them joined hands. Kevin spoke an incantation. They sank beneath the street. Beneath the earth. Gone in a flash.

I stared at the spot where they'd stood for a long moment, until Stacy and Scott walked up behind me. Scott handed me the keys to the Explorer.

Stacy forced a smile. "Where are we headed?"

"You're going to drive to the nearest hospital, because Melody's gonna need trauma care as soon as possible." She might need more than that. Whatever it cost—money, magic, sweat, tears—I'd make it happen.

She was broken, and maybe she couldn't be fixed. But she deserved a chance. I'd do whatever I needed to allow that. She was not nothing. She was a person. She was enough.

She'd have to live with what she'd done. She'd need help with that, too.

"The hospital, okay," Scott said. "Then what?"

"Then you wait there until it happens," I said.

She cocked her head. "Until what happens?"

CHAPTER 17

MALEK REFUSED TO LEAVE Amy until Beth arrived and swore on her life to stay until he returned.

When he opened the door to the shop, the overhead bell rang and heavy metal assaulted my eardrums, overpowering the squeak of my sneakers on the shiny floor and the click of the dog's nails and rush of my own blood inside my head.

He led me into the back and motioned for me to sit down while he prepped his tools. The scent of disinfectant helped me feel clean again. The coolness of the vinyl chair bathed in air conditioning calmed my nerves, but only a little.

The magic we were about to do would change everything.

I didn't want to watch Malek take the blood from his arm that would make the inks come alive, so I averted my eyes. But I couldn't help but hear the guttural sounds he made in his throat—the only sounds he could make at all—while he prayed over the equipment and the colors.

I felt the prayer with my heart. I joined it with all the strength of my will.

What was old, made new again
What came before, brought back again

Never shall the demon come again

May the destroyer in this human heart be healed.

I peeled off my shirt. My favorite shirt of all the Hawaiians, caked in blood and I didn't want to know what else. I balled it up and tossed it in the corner trashcan.

Malek took a disposable razor to my back and shaved the fine hairs, clearing the way for the spell. He wiped the skin down with alcohol and tapped me on the shoulder.

I'm going to draw from memory. The city. The spirit of the city.

No pattern on a sheet of tracing paper. Nothing set in stone. Living spirit couldn't be quantified.

"Go," I said. But he had one more thing to tell me.

No charge.

A lie. A great big, whopping one. I'd pay the price every day for the rest of my life.

He pulled on a pair of black gloves and buzzed the needle to life. Dipped it in the jar of black ink and started the outline. I settled into the pain, feeling the spark of my seer's intuition return with every moment, my magic twining with Malek's, granting the spell greater power. Greater potential.

I poured my love into it, and the city answered that love with its own.

Malek worked for hours. Sweat ran down his face. He wiped it with a towel, cleaned his hands, and kept on. Not once did I pass out, or run to the bathroom to boot, or complain. Not once did I speak a word.

Not until he finished.

Not until the city had been recreated in all its original spirit. In the form it'd been before Melody's spell had sent everything spinning sideways.

He sprayed down my back and wiped it clean again before covering it with a surgical dressing and pulling off his gloves.

The ink is on an accelerated timeline. Effective by the time you walk out the door.

Which meant that even as we spoke, the city was putting itself back together again.

"Thanks, dude."

I don't agree with what you've done for Melody.

"I don't care."

It's not justice.

"It is to me. You wanted something more, you should've been more specific in your demands."

Next time, I will be.

"There won't be a next time if I can help it."

Malek shook his head. *Good luck with that.*

I'd always been lucky. I almost said as much, but the words caught in my throat. I might still be able to rely on luck to get me through, but that wasn't enough anymore. I reached for something that fit the Rudolph Diamond Davies I was now.

"I'm not an apprentice anymore." Saying the words out loud made them real.

You're a full-fledged faery seer, Malek signed.

I shook my head. "It's more than that. Don't you feel it?"

Something's coming.

"Something big. A fight like none of us has ever seen. I can taste it like it's on the tip of my tongue, but I can't say yet what it is. I'll know soon, though."

Malek held my gaze. *You understand now what being a seer really is.*

It didn't mean being able to see beings from other realms with my physical and magical eyes, or holding the laws, or keeping order. Or rather, it didn't mean *only* those things. "I'll be able to see the future."

The possible futures.

Nothing was set in stone. People had free will. They had good intentions and inner demons and the choices they made—what mattered to them, who they loved, whether to act or turn away— would make all the difference in the world.

I stood up, knees popping and muscles stiff. My back ached like hell. "I made a promise to Kev to look after Amy. I know you're taking that on, but I'm gonna help you with it."

He held my gaze. *She'll heal in time.*

I hoped so. "She won't have to do it alone."

He nodded. *Get out of here. Go home.*

He'd be headed over to relieve Beth. I trusted him to do that. I trusted him, period. And I wasn't afraid of him anymore. I respected him. And I understood the difference.

"See you tomorrow." I whistled for Zach to follow.

We stepped out into the morning sun. The street shone with fresh rain. The smell of salt air blown in from the Gulf filled my lungs. Zach wagged his tail.

A cab drove past, spewing exhaust. And a line of cars filled with people on the early commute. Men shuffled out of the leather bar across the street, got on their bikes, and roared out of the lot. They looked exhausted. I wondered if they'd sleep for a week.

I realized I had no idea what day it was.

My cell rang. I'd practically forgotten I had a phone.

I pulled it from the cargo pocket of my shorts and answered.

"Rude?" my father asked.

I blew out a breath I'd been holding my whole life. "Who else would it be?"

"You coming home for breakfast?"

"Right now."

"There's bacon," he said, and hung up.

I hit the appropriate button on my keychain with a trembling finger. The Explorer's door locks flipped up. I put Zach in the passenger seat and climbed in behind the wheel. Started the engine and flicked the turn signal to let the traffic know I planned to join them. To join the rhythm of the city.

The ink on my back writhed in response to my thought. The magic and the city would live with me. Live in me.

As long as we took care of each other, we would live.

If you enjoyed this book, please consider leaving a review. It doesn't have to be long—even a few words will be very appreciated.

Reviews make it possible for an author to continue writing books in a series. They make a big difference in helping to get the word out about a book or a series. And reviews can make the all difference in the world when a reader wants to take a chance on a new author, but isn't sure whether they will like the book.

Thank you for taking hours out of your busy life to read. I hope this book brought you time to escape into a story, and that it brought you joy.

Turn the page to read Chapter 1 of the third book in *The Faery Chronicles* series, **Faery Sovereign.**

LESLIE CLAIRE WALKER

Faery Sovereign

THE FAERY CHRONICLES
BOOK THREE

FAERY SOVEREIGN - CHAPTER 1

THE TWILIGHT felt charged, electric enough to raise the hairs on my arms. Doug fir and hemlock, their enormous trunks furred with moss, stretched higher than I could see. The crow that had been following me cawed on an overhead branch, taking off in a flutter of feathers and a shower of sap and needles. Its shadow flowed over me like dark water, then wheeled away to the north, leaving me alone in the Faery wood, the Forest of Dreams.

Forest of Nightmares was more like it.

My name is Kevin Landon. Once upon a time, I was a human living in the human world. By day, I went to school, studying my ass off and angling for a college scholarship to a school far, far away. By night, I served as a go-between among fae and humans. Magic allowed me to hear other people's thoughts when things got danger-ous. I didn't like it, because all I'd ever wanted to be was normal, but you couldn't wish away reality, could you?

If you'd asked my greatest fear, I'd have told you it was that I'd go too far over the edge into magic. Lose my humanity.

Then a girl I knew cast a spell that turned my city of Houston, Texas into a burnt-out shell of its former self. The office towers downtown looked like a bomb had gone off—steel frames bent and twisted, glass windows shattered all over the streets and sidewalks, concrete crumbled. Most of four-and-a-half-million people vanished without a trace. They were the lucky ones.

The ones who remained were transformed into the things that terrified them most, including me. White-feathered fae wings grew out of my back and my senses became super strong. My emotions turned up to an ear-splitting, mind-numbing, heartbreaking volume.

We'd averted an apocalypse, but we hadn't been able to return everything and everyone to what they'd been before the spell. My best friend Rude was supposed to be working on that, but we had no way to contact him, so no way to know how that was going.

That was two weeks ago. This was now.

Insects buzzed in the trees and low over the soil. Flies with bright blue wingtips, dragonflies as big as swallows, and other bugs I didn't recognize. Frogs croaked in a strange harmony that seemed more like speech than song. I felt sure they were talking about me.

I took the last sip from my steel water bottle, tilting the bottle vertical to suck down the last of the liquid. The flat-topped stone I sat on rocked as I shifted my weight. I imagined it felt the same as me, unstable and wondering what the hell I was doing there, disturbing its ordinary life. The dying embers of the fire in of me glowed like dragon's eyes. A few fat drops of rain fell, pelting my head and hands, and hissed when they struck the heat.

The mossy earth where I'd slept beside Simone had almost regained its spring and shape, as if we'd never been there at all. My brown leather pack rested beside hers—his and hers. Except we weren't exactly a couple. I didn't know what we were, and she wasn't here—a fact that was seriously freaking me out.

She'd gone to get water an hour ago, and she'd insisted on going alone. She had more experience in Faery than I did. She knew what she was doing, and she'd be all right. She didn't need me watching over her like she was some fragile thing. She'd said all of that, raising her voice with each word, as if she was trying to convince not just me, but herself.

She had a complicated history with humanity. She'd grown up

human, but she had a talent unlike anyone else's. Her voice mesmer-ized. She could make people whatever she wanted them to. The Faery King wanted her for his own, so he'd marked her. She slowly became fae.

No one could refuse her golden voice. They not only felt what she wanted them to feel, they acted on those feelings. She could read people, too. Just one sound was all it took for her to have a lock on their hopes, fears, and desires.

The spell that destroyed the city, giving life to everyone's fears, made her human again. Whether that change was permanent remained to be seen.

She didn't want me to treat her like she was fragile, but she was newly breakable in a realm of magic, and she should've returned from the river a half hour ago.

The rain hesitated, the clouds far overhead not yet ready to let go completely. Wind gusted from the west, pregnant with ozone. I took a deep breath. It didn't stop the sharp claws of panic digging into my gut.

There were worse things in Faery than the potential for hypothermia after a thunderstorm. There were worse things than death. There were… things.

No matter what Simone wanted, I shouldn't have let her go alone.

I slammed the water bottle into the earth, my frustration and improved strength digging the base two inches into the soil. Pushing to my feet, I said a quick prayer that the campsite would remain safe and undiscovered by anyone other than Simone and me. I was still new to the power that came with being fae, but I was getting good at camouflage.

I forced myself to take a deep breath. On the exhale, I imagined the space behind my heart opening and connecting the well of life force in the realm of Faery, the energy from which all life in Faery—and all the other worlds—was created. That connection was the heart of what I was now. No longer just myself, but part of something bigger.

From my first step along the route to the river, the firs and hemlocks read and understood my intention, where I needed to go.

They *moved* to guide me, literally. The forest blurred around me. The air vibrated so hard, I could almost see the molecules of magic it was made of. Then a clear path appeared between the trees, the loam along the way subtly lit.

My steps felt sure, stepping over fallen limbs and seeking roots—more sure than they'd ever been on the cracked concrete sidewalks back home. I picked up the pace, covering the distance as if I were running.

Simone didn't have the same help from the forest or the same connection with it. Chances were, I'd find her in a minute or two with nothing more than a twisted ankle. I was only freaking myself out, blowing the situation out of proportion. She'd be all right, but moving slowly, or resting somewhere inconspicuous. It wasn't like she could text or call. Magic didn't mix well with phones.

Instinct spoke, a still, small voice in the back of my mind.

Hide.

The muscles in my shoulders contracted on their own, pulling my wings tighter against my back as I ducked behind the wide trunk of a fir. A twig snapped, cracking the air like a gunshot. I held my breath as a drop of rain landed on the bridge of my nose and slid down slow, trickling off the tip.

Three heavy, stumbling footfalls crunched on fallen needles. Underneath that cacophony, a moan of pain rose in a familiar, mesmerizing voice.

A single word bloomed in my mind like a poisoned flower. *Knife.*

It was a thought. Simone's, not mine. She was in danger, and she was broadcasting in the hope that I'd hear. My heart climbed into my throat.

They're close.

Just those two words. Nothing about who or what had attacked her.

Instinct screamed that I shouldn't move an inch. Stay hidden or die.

Simone was in trouble.

I broke cover as she staggered out of the brush, a flash of peacock feather halter-top and leather pants. She tripped over her feet and fell face-first, unable to get her arms in front of her to break momentum. I lunged and caught her by the shoulders, tucked my hands under her arms, and dragged her behind the fir. Her toes grooved the soil, which would point the enemy straight at us.

The forest hushed, suddenly still and silent. The insects and frogs didn't so much as whisper. The wind held its breath. The rush of my blood inside my head pulsed and roared like an oncoming freight train.

I couldn't see Simone's face through the tangle of long purple and black hair, but I could smell the stink of fear that rolled off of her in waves and taste the coppery blood that dripped from scratches on her arms, along with the deeper, richer scent of blood from a more substantial wound. I pulled her to her knees, where she swayed before she caught her balance. Only then did I let go long enough to brush the hair from her face.

Her eyes were wide, her voice pitched low. "The girl. She followed me. She—shit!"

The fine hairs on the back of my neck rose like antennae a split-second before lightning pain exploded in my right shoulder.

The world turned gray and grainy, then color flooded in again. I spun and—whoosh—something cut the air where my head had been. I glimpsed a wiry arm. A blade arced into a silver blur.

I knocked it out of the air, the edge slicing open my forearm before it dropped. Simone grabbed the hilt, scrambling away.

The attacker shoved me off my feet with supernatural strength. I crashed into the fir's truck, sliding down like a ton of bricks, the impact stealing my breath. She was on me before I could roll, punching me twice before I could raise an arm to defend. Even then, I couldn't block everything she threw. There was magic in her blows. And deadly intent. Every blow felt like a killing strike.

I reached with one hand for anything I could use as a weapon, but found only leaves and needles and dirt. I stretched, fingertips brushing something smooth and cool and hard. A stone. It tipped toward me, but not enough to grab.

The girl's fist collided with my left temple. The force of the blow rocked me to the core. Nausea exploded in my gut. Consciousness felt light as a feather, ready to fly away.

I reached for the stone again, focusing with every ounce of will I had. It tipped into my palm. I gripped it tight and swung for the girl's head, connecting with a solid crack. She shook it off. I swung a second time, harder.

The rain of fists stopped. She blinked at me, sucking air.

I bucked her off of me, drawing in my legs and kicking her hard enough to send her flying onto her back. I rolled to a crouch, dizzy and sick, black fae blood streaming into my eyes as she pushed up onto her elbows.

Tangled waves of brown hair brushed her freckled shoulders. The tips of her ears were pointed, and the gauzy tops of wings stretched at disjointed angles behind her. If she were human, I'd peg her age at thirteen, but she wasn't human and never had been.

She stared at me as if I were prey, her skin so pale I could see the dark pulse of blood in the veins at her temples. She tried to rise, but her arms refused to hold her. Her eyes widened and her mouth opened in a round O. A heartbeat later, she collapsed on her side like a deflating balloon.

I waited for a fake-out—if this were a horror movie, she'd get up again when I least expected it. But she didn't move again, not even to breathe.

I pulled in a lungful of air, trying to understand what had just happened. Only one thing I was sure of: it should be me on the ground dead, not her.

The crackle of twigs and needles behind me had me wheeling meet the next danger, but there was only Simone on all fours, closing the small distance between us. She held the attacker's knife in one tight fist.

"Kevin, get away from her. If she's sick, she's contagious to fae."

I shook my head. "She's not like the others we've run into. She was so strong. Stronger than any fae ought to be."

I duck-walked the few feet to her side and pushed one shoulder to settle her on her back. Her sightless brown eyes looked like empty glass. I reached to close them.

At my touch, the darkness I'd seen in the veins at her temples brightened, the shine fading to a plain, empty white. Spiral markings of the same white rose to the surface of her skin.

I yanked my hand back. "Damn."

The same spell that made me fae and turned Simone human had infected the fae world like a virus. We knew it spread, but hadn't yet determined how. We knew it was fatal, but had no metric for how long it took to kill. It took away the will to live. It turned magic against the magician.

"Every other sick fae we've seen got those as soon as the disease took hold," I said. "The hell is going on here?"

"Kevin, back away, please."

"She punched me bloody. Pretty sure I've been exposed."

"Don't joke about this."

I held up both hands as a sign of truce. "How did she find you?"

"I saw her in the woods on the way to the water."

"Did she see you?"

"I didn't think so, but I was wrong, wasn't I? She was hunting me, Kev."

Hunting. I felt cold at the thought.

The girl's hand twitched. I jumped an inch off the ground, landing on my ass. "You see that?"

Simone nodded. "Look at her skin."

Vapor rose from the girl, and her skin began to dry and crack, thinning as we watched, as if it were made of old paper. The wind picked up, lifting tufts of the girl's hair and tearing them from her scalp as easy as plucking flowers from the ground, the breeze carrying away strands like dandelion fluff.

My own skin began to crawl.

The girl's body began to shrink, sinking in on itself as if the flesh and blood and bone that gave it mass were wasting away. For the space of a breath, the air stank of rotting meat, then the stench vanished. Her fingers began to curl, her arms to roll up like a carpet for whom no one had anymore use. Her feet and legs followed. It was like something out of a cartoon, except it was real and right in front of us and terrifying.

Bile fountained into my mouth. I swallowed hard to keep from throwing up.

Simone's face paled. "God."

My voice shook. "You ever seen anything like that?"

She shook her head. "The other sick fae—they didn't do this after they died. This is something else. Something different."

"Something to erase any trace of who she was or why she came here."

"Why do you say that?"

"I don't know." I hadn't been thinking anything like that before I opened my mouth. I started to speak again, but it took two tries before I could articulate what needed to come out. "Even after people die, it takes a while for their bodies to really shut down. The blood's not pumping and the nervous system's not jumping, but there's still a kind of fading life there. Someone who knew what they were doing could use that to get information, kind of like you can still get DNA from a dead person, only with magic. Am I making sense?"

She nodded. "You're saying that she, or whoever sent her, set up some kind of self-destruct mechanism in case she died."

"Yeah, that's what I'm saying."

"You sound like a crazy person, Kevin."

No way around it—she was right. "Yep."

Simone rose to her feet. "Up. Turn around. Let me look at your shoulder."

I stood. "What about the cut on your stomach?"

"It's nothing."

"It didn't smell like nothing."

She made a face. "Kevin, that's gross. Anyway, if I say it's fine, it's fine."

I wanted to push, but her tone slammed the door shut on any further questions.

"Your shoulder is also gross."

"Sorry. I don't feel anything. It's like I wasn't even stabbed."

I couldn't see her roll her eyes, but I felt it all the same. "Must be adrenaline."

"The fae have adrenaline?"

"It's not that, but it's like that. Your body creates a kind of magical patch that blunts the effects of losing your darkness."

"It keeps my blood on the inside."

"So to speak. I can't see it well enough. Off with the stupid shirt, Kevin."

The one I insisted on wearing even though I'd had to cut holes in the back for my wings. Without the cotton covering my skin, I felt unguarded, too open—naked.

When her fingertips brushed my skin, they seemed to burn. I couldn't tell whether that was because of my heightened fae sensation, or because of how I felt about Simone. I blew out a long breath to disguise the intensity of the sensation and hoped she wouldn't notice.

She seemed one-hundred percent focused on my shoulder wound. "It doesn't look that bad."

The words should've comforted, but they gave me a shiver instead. "What aren't you telling me?"

"I don't know. Something about it feels wrong."

"You can't tell what it is?"

"No. We should get out of here. Whoever sent that girl will know by now that she didn't kill you."

"You mean 'us.'"

"I'm not anything for an enemy to worry about, Kev."

That wasn't true at all. I shook my head. "You know things no human could know. You still have the power of your voice."

"It's not the same. I'm just human now," she said. "You're not only fae, you're special. The King was afraid of you. He ruined your life. He kidnapped your friends and family."

That was how I'd ended up acting as an intermediary between humans and fae in the first place. The magic had risen inside me without warning, transforming me from a bereaved nerd in search of a scholarship to the first faraway school that would take me to an outright freak accused of murder, thrust into the secret hidden beneath the surface of the normal world. Magic was real. The fae walked among us. They considered me a danger, turning my life upside down, all because the Faery King believed I would someday take him down.

"He never tried to kill me, Simone."

"Because he believes you're important to the Faery realm itself. He's an asshole, but he's not willing to risk an entire world."

I didn't want to talk about the finer points of the King's douchebaggery. I didn't care about his reasons except for how they affected me and the people I loved. "My point is, this isn't him sending an assassin after me."

Her eyes widened.

My heart stuttered in my chest. "What did I say?"

"Assassin."

I furrowed my brow. "I was being sarcastic about that, sort of."

She shook her head. "There's so much you don't know."

"I'm aware. So, tell me."

"Walk, and I'll tell you. We need to get back to camp as fast as possible. Then we need to get the hell out of Faery."

I took a step in the direction of camp. The air vibrated. The trees *moved* once again, ready to guide me where I wanted to go, safely and easily.

Simone shuddered. "Good thing this forest is friendly."

"Yeah. What about assassins?"

"Magical assassins."

"You're kidding."

"Wish I was. There's an entire order. They take in kids whose magic manifests when they're super young. They train them to use their power to kill."

"How young?"

"Anywhere between five and ten years old."

"Jesus." I couldn't even imagine what it would've been like for my magic to rise when I was that little, with no way to explain how I felt or how scared I was, with no way to understand it or to even find someone who could help me. "This order, it takes them from their families?"

"Sometimes. Sometimes their families kick them out or institutionalize them, and the order picks the up off the street or from the hospital. No one else is looking out for those kids. The law can't help them. The cops don't even know about magic—the real cops, not the ones the King sent after you. Magic is a secret, Kevin."

"Because we hide it. Because we're afraid of what other people would do if they found out."

"No, Kev. Because it protects itself. Normal people don't even see it. If by some chance they've got some innate magical talent or ability and catch a glimpse, they'll find a way to discount what they've seen or felt, or make up a story so that what happened makes sense in the normal world. These kids are at the order's mercy."

Every word she said felt horribly true. "The dead girl isn't human. She's definitely fae. She had a fae sickness."

"That she could've caught when she arrived in Faery."

It made sense—if the girl was really what Simone thought she was. "Does the order take fae kids?"

"The fae and the angels and demons guard their offspring more closely. The worlds they inhabit are magic to the core. The chance that the order could take one of their kids is slim, and the risk they'd take in terms of violence and payback is too great. But the order has been known to take human children and…change them."

Like I'd been changed. Like Simone had been changed. "Her strength. The force behind her punches."

Simone nodded. "I think the girl is from the order. The question is, who hired them to kill you?"

I could see the girl in my mind's eye, arriving in Faery through a portal, the sickness striking her like a fist to the chest, mucking up her magic, her thoughts, and her body. I could hear her breathing change, heart beating too fast, and feel how even the act of stalking our campsite set the muscles in her thighs quivering like gelatin. My mind filled with her thoughts.

Neither the woman nor her target was as on-guard as we should be. Easy prey.

If she waited until nightfall, or until we slept, she could complete her mission and get back home, where her mentor could tell her in clear words what was suddenly wrong with her, where the Order could drive away the dread that settled in the pit of her belly. But then the woman had left camp, heading for the river, and that presented a perfect opportunity to take out the one person who stood in her way.

When the woman didn't return in time, the target would become distracted with worry. He'd forget his magic, make stupid decisions. He'd be easier to pick off. It was only a matter of time before—

Simone's voice broke my concentration. "Kevin, what are you doing?"

I stared at her, a chill overtaking me.

"Your fae intuition again?"

Maybe. No. Yes. "At first, I saw her, and then I saw us through her eyes, as if I were thinking her thoughts. I could feel the sickness take hold. And…"

"And what?"

"She was expecting backup."

"If she doesn't report in, how long before the order sends someone after her?"

"I didn't get that far," I said. "We shouldn't go back to camp at all."

"I want our stuff."

"If her backup arrives while we're there, we might not get lucky again. We can get more stuff."

She threaded the blade through her belt. "I left something there that we can't replace."

"What kind of something?"

"Later, okay?"

She would tell me in her own good time or not at all. "Okay."

We walked for a few minutes in silence. I kept my physical ears peeled for sounds that shouldn't be there. The huff of someone else's breathing. The rustle of brush or branch between gusts of wind. I kept my psychic ears primed, too, imagining them like satellite dishes waiting to pick up any semblance of a stray thought that didn't belong to Simone or me.

I didn't hear a thing.

The campsite looked just like I'd left it. The embers had cooled. Only a wisp of smoke rose from the center of the ash.

Simone grabbed her pack and took a step away from me for privacy, peeling open the flap and sticking her face inside. Whatever she'd wanted to grab was in the pack, and she'd been worried that it would disappear, or that someone would take it.

"Everything's good?" I asked, picking up my own pack and shrugging into it.

Her shoulders climbed towards her ears. "Fine. Everything's exactly where it's supposed to be."

"Then why are you tensing up?"

She slowly lowered the bag, hanging on to it by her fingertips. She looked at me with unfocused eyes. "I don't feel right."

I took the bag from her, slipping my head and shoulder through the strap. She opened her mouth to argue, then snapped it shut. She splayed her fingers, raising her arms as if she were trying to grab the air around her for balance.

"Hold on to me," I said.

She gripped the waist of my jeans while I reached for the hem of her halter, dragging it up to lay eyes on the shallow cut to her belly.

She hadn't been playing off the damage. It looked exactly as she'd advertised—except for the faint shine of magic around the wound, as if someone had sprayed it with a red mist.

Her voice sounded small and faraway. "I feel like I'm going to pass out again."

A heartbeat later, her legs gave way.

I pulled her close, holding her weight with one arm as the hairs on the back of my neck sprang to attention.

Trouble was close again, whether it was a second assassin or something else. We had only a minute or two before it was on us. Fear spiked in my gut, clawing its way up and out, tightening every nerve to the breaking point. If I didn't do something—if I didn't do the right thing—things would get bloody.

I gathered the anxiety rising inside me and focused it like a laser, drawing my magic around it like a coiled serpent ready to strike. I loosed it through my free hand, drawing a portal to take us through. The stink of sulfur bloomed all around us as the doorway opened into the In-Between, the moisture in the air heating until it bubbled and burst.

My strength ebbed as the portal formed. Drawing the doorway shouldn't have drained me so quickly. I didn't have an endless reserve of fae magic, but I had enough. The brighter the portal grew, the weaker I felt.

I hitched Simone up and over my shoulder so I could run with her if it came to that. Stepping through the portal, I whispered a prayer that the realm between worlds would shelter us. That the predators chasing us here wouldn't be able to track us there.

If I didn't find somewhere safe to go to ground, we might not make it through the night.

That wasn't fear talking. It was fae instinct, which meant that it was true.

ALSO BY LESLIE CLAIRE WALKER

THE AWAKENED MAGIC SAGA

THE SOUL FORGE

(The Complete Series)

Angel Hunts

Angel Rises

Angel Falls

Angel Strikes

Angel Roars

Angel Burns

THE FAERY CHRONICLES

(The Complete Series)

Faery Novice

Faery Prophet

Faery Sovereign

SHORT STORY COLLECTIONS

Ink & Blood

Ink & Stars

Ink & Sword

ABOUT THE AUTHOR

Since the age of seven, Leslie Claire Walker has wanted to be Princess Leia—wise and brave and never afraid of a fight, no matter the odds.

Leslie hails from the concrete and steel canyons and lush bayous of southeast Texas—a long way from Alderaan. Now, she lives in the rain-drenched Pacific Northwest with a cast of spectacular characters, including cats, harps, fantastic pieces of art that may or may not be doorways to other realms, and too many fantasy novels to count.

She is the author of **The Faery Chronicles** and **Soul Forge** series, two complete series of urban fantasy novels, novellas, and stories filled with found family, angels, assassins, faeries, and demons.

Connect with Leslie
leslieclairewalker.com
leslie@leslieclairewalker.com